An
Improbable Fiction

A RINEHART SUSPENSE NOVEL

A RINEHART SUSPENSE NOVEL

An Improbable ❧ Fiction ❧

BY

Sara Woods

HOLT, RINEHART AND WINSTON
New York   Chicago   San Francisco

Any work of fiction whose characters were of a uniform excellence would rightly be condemned—by that fact if by no other—as being incredibly dull. Therefore no excuse can be considered necessary for the villainy or folly of the people in this book. It seems extremely unlikely that any one of them should resemble a real person alive or dead. Any such resemblance is completely unintentional and without malice.

Library of Congress Catalog Number: 78-138880

First Edition

SBN: 03-085088-6

Printed in the United States of America

Contents

THURSDAY, *1st February*   1

FRIDAY, *2nd February*   5

SATURDAY, *3rd February*   14

WEDNESDAY, *7th February*   23

THURSDAY, *8th February*   38

THURSDAY, *29th February*   60

FRIDAY, *1st March*   66

SATURDAY, *2nd March*   87

MONDAY, *4th March*   102

TUESDAY, *5th March*   114

THURSDAY, *7th March*   117

FRIDAY, *8th March*   123

SATURDAY, *9th March*   137

SUNDAY, *10th March*   146

MONDAY, *11th March*   149

TUESDAY, *12th March*   176

If this were played upon a stage now, I could condemn it as an improbable fiction.

TWELFTH NIGHT, Act III, Sc. iv.

An
Improbable Fiction

A RINEHART SUSPENSE NOVEL

Indefinably, the duckling was an ugly duckling. Antony Maitland was looking at it upside down, but for whatever reason his uncle had desired his presence it was not to obtain a criticism of his artistic ability. "If the case may be said to have any advantage at all," said Sir Nicholas Harding coldly, "it is that of being unusual."

"Billing *versus* Travis-Hartley (1872)," Maitland hazarded, coming round the desk to stand near the fire. He sounded casual, but there was a suggestion of wariness in his eyes.

"So far as my information goes, the facts are in no way analogous," Sir Nicholas told him. And then, in a slightly less lofty tone, one that could even have been called querulous, "I can't think why you wanted to take it on."

"Mallory had already accepted the papers."

"At young Willett's instigation, no doubt."

Maitland smiled. "You're wrong about that, sir. Willett gets his effects in a much more subtle way."

I

"Still, you won't deny he has your interests—what he thinks are your interests—at heart."

"If he has, it's just as well. Mallory has no respect for me at all."

Sir Nicholas removed a careful inch of ash from his cigar. "We have established, then, that you were not averse to acting."

"Have we?" But what was the use of arguing, after all. "The thing is, you see, Uncle Nick, Johnny Lund is the solicitor."

"Lund? Lund?" said Sir Nicholas, deliberately vague.

"Of course you remember," Maitland informed him, only a little too patiently. "Jenny thinks—"

"So now we're getting to it!"

"Well, to be honest, I'd like to help him too. He's a nice lad, and you must admit he's taken on a difficult job here."

"There seems to be no reason why you, too, should involve yourself in an impossible situation."

"I haven't seen the girl yet. She may prove more reasonable when I talk to her."

"What woman ever did?" inquired Sir Nicholas disagreeably.

"You've acted in libel cases yourself before now."

"So I have. In general, you know, there is a good deal of room for maneuver, but what have you here?"

"A girl who says her sister was murdered," said Maitland, rather annoyingly replying to a question that was intended to be merely rhetorical.

"When the coroner said, quite plainly, that she committed suicide," Sir Nicholas added. "Besides, that isn't all she says." His tone could hardly have been more accusing if his nephew had himself been responsible for the situation they were discussing.

"No, she says Paul Granville did the killing."

"A man who is a public figure . . . a popular entertainer . . . and as such in a position to prove damages—"

"It's all very dreadful, Uncle Nick."

"—and as if that weren't enough she refuses both to rescind her statement and to contemplate any alternative defense."

2

"We couldn't deny what she said; too many people heard her. We couldn't say it wasn't defamatory; murder's a serious business, even today. We can't claim privilege—"

"You could suggest it was fair comment . . . it is certainly in the public interest that a murderer should be exposed. And that's another thing," said Sir Nicholas, following some train of thought of his own, "a female journalist. I didn't know you were so fond of the representatives of the press."

Maitland frowned at that, but he seemed to be giving the statement his attention. "I'd be the first to admit they can be troublesome," he said. "If she turns out to be one of those hard-boiled women . . . but I've acted for clients before with whom I wasn't personally in sympathy."

"Well, I suppose you've made up your mind."

For a moment they regarded each other: two tall men with a certain likeness between them that was one of expression only; in other respects they were as dissimilar as could be. Sir Nicholas was fair, his features far more regular than those of his nephew, his manner unconsciously authoritative where the younger man was casual. "I think I'm committed, sir," said Maitland at last. "Johnny made rather a point of it."

"How does he come to be representing the girl? It seems only yesterday you were going to see him at school."

"He's in his middle twenties now, Uncle Nick. He's been qualified for three years, and he's with Bellerby's firm."

"In a junior capacity, no doubt. So that he gets all the clients no one else wants."

"Something like that," Maitland agreed. "Bellerby said 'It will be good experience for the boy,' "—unconsciously he mimicked the solicitor's hearty tone—"but I think more likely he considered giving the case to Johnny a sure way of involving me."

"Your special talents," agreed Sir Nicholas sourly. "He must be the only man in the world to welcome your meddling." But his attention was beginning to wander. He reached out a hand and patted the document he had been perusing when his nephew came in. "There would have been a brief for you from

3

Wattersons if you weren't tied up with this other business," he said.

"Derek will do just as well." (He thought, but did not add, "And with a lot less argument.") Looking down at the desk he could see more clearly now the latest detachment of ducks that his uncle had been sketching, with the ugly duckling standing a little aloof. "Is that the case where the old boy left everything to his nurse?" he asked. "And the family are contesting the will?"

"It is."

"Who are you acting for?"

"The nurse," sighed Sir Nicholas. "She is an uncommonly ill-favored woman." He drew a circle round the solitary duck, emphasizing the point.

"That ought to be a help rather than a hindrance."

"In what way?"

It was Maitland's turn to be vague. "Undue influence," he said. "From what you say it's unlikely her patient fell in love with her, at least."

"Are you proposing that I should point that out to the court?"

"No need to say anything. They'll see for themselves if she has a face like the back of a bus."

"I am grateful, of course, for your interest, but I should prefer to conduct the case on more orthodox lines," said Sir Nicholas repressively. But he added, as his nephew made for the door, "I admit the point had not occurred to me. I must consider whether I cannot turn it to some advantage."

John Lund was a good-looking young man, with fair hair and a hefty pair of shoulders. He had a rather quiet, serious manner, and an attractive smile, and he ushered his client into Maitland's room in chambers as if she were something rare and fragile; which Maitland observed with some amusement . . . the girl was not quite what he expected, but she certainly didn't look as if she were made of porcelain.

What had he expected, anyway? He might have known she'd be pretty, a girl who got even casual employment on television must have something in the way of looks. Dark hair, straight and shining, and either unfashionably long or unfashionably short, he wasn't sure which. Brown eyes, with a rather uncomfortable directness, an appealing mouth, a square chin. She was a beauty all right, but she might be a tartar for all that.

They were both seated now, looking at him hopefully. "I want to hear the whole story again from you, Miss Edison, if you don't mind."

5

"Well—"

"Imagine you're telling it for the first time . . . that I know nothing about you, or your sister, or even about Paul Granville."

She chose to take him at his word. "My name is Lynn Edison. I work—I worked for the *Courier*, and I used to do a weekly commentary for the *Wessex* television network." (Wasn't she a little young for that? Much the same age as Johnny, or perhaps a year or two older if her self-assurance was anything to go by.) "The paper wouldn't put out the story I wanted—well, I didn't expect them to—so I added it to my broadcast on the twenty-fourth of January. I said, 'The death of Cynthia Edison has been dismissed as suicide, whereas in fact it was murder, deliberate and premeditated, and not by some person unknown but by someone well known to all of you. Paul Granville.' And then I stopped, because I saw they'd cut me off the air."

"You must forgive me if I tell you I'm not altogether surprised."

Lynn gave him a quick smile, rather as though acknowledging a pleasantry she didn't really understand. Johnny said in gloomy exaggeration, "A billion people must have heard her. But the evidence of the people who were monitoring the broadcast is all they need, of course."

"They don't even need that, I'm afraid, unless Miss Edison can be persuaded—"

"I won't deny I said it."

"Obviously not. It wouldn't do any good."

"Well, I won't apologize, either, if that's what you mean."

"It might help matters if you did."

"I know, and you'd tack on a sort of explanation. 'Overwrought by her sister's death—' No, and no, and no!"

"I told you," said Johnny.

"So you did. We are to proceed then with one defense only, that of justification. How are we to justify what you said, Miss Edison?"

6

"My sister was killed."

"That was not the finding of the coroner's court."

"But it was all so—so perfunctory. For instance, they asked me to identify her, and that was all."

"It didn't occur to you then to accuse Paul Granville?"

"I never got the chance." She said this fiercely, as though daring him to comment. "I went to the police afterwards, of course, but they'd made up their minds by then."

"I see. Tell me about your sister's death."

"She'd taken half a bottle of some tablets called *Drowse,* dissolved in black coffee so far as anyone could tell. She drank it, and went to sleep, and she just never woke up."

"And why do you think it was murder?"

His casual tone did nothing to placate her. "I know it was!"

"How do you know then?" he asked patiently.

"Because she never took things like that. She wouldn't have them in the house." She paused, glaring at him. "She had a friend who got hooked on drugs, if you want to know, and she was terrified it would happen to her."

"That might be an argument against accident—"

"No, because you see—the police told me this much—she'd taken only half a bottle, but the one beside her was empty. If she'd gone out and bought one she'd either have taken more, or there'd have been some left in the bottle."

He said, "I see," again, and drew out the words in a doubtful way.

"If you don't believe me—" said Lynn.

"I was thinking that it would be quite easy for a person determined on suicide to get hold of a partly-full bottle of—what did you say?—*Drowse.*"

"Isn't that a little farfetched?" she asked scornfully.

"I don't think so." He smiled at her. "If we grant you're right about that, what about the next point? Why should Paul Granville have killed her?"

"I don't know. I read somewhere that motive doesn't matter, in law."

7

"This isn't a murder trial. It will matter to you, all right, when you're trying to prove——"

"Well then, he was tired of her. It must have been that."

"I'm afraid I shall have to ask you to amplify that statement a little, Miss Edison."

"They weren't living together. It wasn't that sort of—of semi-official arrangement. But I think he paid for her flat, and I know he went there often."

"To spend the night?"

"That's what I meant."

"Was this—this arrangement, you said—generally known?"

"I don't think so. Paul has a very pure image, you know. It would have been bad enough if he'd got married. Any sort of irregularity would have been fatal."

"You knew about it."

"I asked her straight out who was paying for the apartment. I knew she couldn't afford Guildford Place out of what she earned. It was a tiny bedsitter really, but a frightfully good address."

"You asked her, and she told you——"

"Just that . . . there was *someone*." The mimicry was savage. "I told her not to be so damned coy, and then she said it was Paul. But she swore me to secrecy first."

"Very well then: you *know* she was murdered, you *know* she was living with Paul Granville, you *think* he was tired of her. That isn't necessarily a reason for murder, you know."

"He might have thought she'd make trouble if he left her."

"What about her own image?" He smiled at her again, but still she did not respond.

"I only said that's what he might have thought."

"You still haven't told me how you know he killed her."

"There was nobody else. She wasn't promiscuous, you know. As long as she and Paul were together——"

"There might have been someone who loved her,"—as he said it, the word sounded oddly old-fashioned—"whom she didn't care about."

8

"There wasn't. I'm sure there wasn't." She sounded shaken, as though this was the first time the idea had occurred to her. "I know Paul was going to be there that night," she said stubbornly. "She told me—"

"What did she say?" he prompted her as she broke off.

"Well, it was just the implication. I thought that was what she meant."

"Let's go back to the question, shall we? How do you know—?"

"I just know it, that's all. Haven't you ever felt something, very strongly, that you couldn't explain?"

He caught Johnny's eye, and gave him a rueful smile. "If you want my advice, Miss Edison," he said, ignoring the question, "you'll let me proffer an apology for you, with any trimmings you like to name."

"I won't!"

"You're asking Mr. Lund to make bricks without straw, you know," said Maitland tritely.

"But that's—" She glanced from one of them to the other, for the first time unsure of herself. "I thought you would help us."

"I shall be acting in court on his instructions," he told her.

"But you've done it before, haven't you? Helped to find out more than appeared on the surface, I mean. Meg told me—"

"Heaven and earth!" said Maitland unemotionally. "Meg Hamilton?"

"Yes, but she's married. Her real name's Farrell now."

He ignored that. "I might have known it." Again he exchanged a look with Johnny Lund. "She told you that if you went to Mr. Bellerby and he saw what kind of a mess you were in, it would be one way of getting in touch with me."

This time she smiled back at him openly. "Something like that. I'm sorry if I've upset you, Mr. Maitland, but I really do need your help, you know."

"You're asking me to prove: first, that your sister was murdered; second, that she was Paul Granville's mistress; third, that he killed her . . . for some reason you can only guess at."

9

"I'm asking a great deal, I know."

"What do you think, Johnny?"

Lund's eyes were on the girl. "I wouldn't know where to start," he said. "So—like Miss Edison—I hope you'll help us."

"I suppose I must. But I don't think we have the faintest hope of succeeding. If I were even sure—"

"Don't you believe me?" That was Lynn, belligerent again.

"I believe that you believe—" A muddle, better start again. "I'm sure you believe what you've told me, but I'm not so sure your judgment is correct."

"I'm not letting prejudice blind me, if that's what you mean."

"But you can't help being prejudiced . . . can you? For instance, why don't you like Paul Granville?"

"Because he . . . isn't my type, that's all."

"No other reason?"

"No."

"You were fond of your sister, weren't you?"

"Very fond." She snapped the words, but then seemed to relent. "If you mean would I rather think she was murdered than that she was unhappy enough to commit suicide . . . yes I would."

"Why?"

"Because I can't bear to think of her being as miserable as that and not telling me. She would have told me, I'm sure. I don't like to think of her being murdered either, but that way she might have gone on being happy . . . right to the end."

"I see. Well, we shall do what we can, Miss Edison . . . Mr. Lund and I. Which brings us to the difficult question of how this case is going to leave you financially."

"I can—" She flushed, and caught herself up on the statement. "I have just under three thousand pounds from my father's will. I've lost my job, of course, so I'm living on that now. Will the damages be very much?"

"If the jury find for the plaintiff they will be substantial, I should think. Is there any chance of Granville accepting—say—a thousand pounds to settle out of court, Johnny?"

"Not a hope."

"Then there is nothing left for us but to hope for the best."

"After all, we may win," Lynn told him.

"You're an optimist, Miss Edison." He hesitated. "How will you live if the newspaper world is closed to you after the trial?"

"I shall get a job as a typist, I suppose. I don't think anyone is likely to employ me in my own line, do you?"

"I'm only surprised the television company haven't been joined with you as defendants."

"Paul wouldn't do that." She was contemptuous again. "He's too nice. He even came to see me."

"Oh, dear!"

He sounded so doleful that she smiled again, this time more freely. "You're quite right, of course, we quarreled, and Danny was there—Daniel Owen, his agent. And I said everything over again, and more, but Mr. Lund tells me that's only slander, while the other was libel, I don't quite see why."

"Mr. Lund would also tell you that since the Defamation Act, 1952, broadcast statements are to be treated as publication in permanent form, as far as the law is concerned."

"Oh, I see." She made a pretty good attempt, he thought, to sound as if she meant it. "Is there anything else you want to know?"

"Paul Granville, for instance. Tell me a little about him."

"But you must know—"

"I saw him—once—in a film. It was not an experience I had any wish to repeat."

"He's very good-looking," she objected, as if that invalidated the whole statement.

"I'm notoriously lacking in taste, but I'll agree with you there."

"And a good actor."

"That also."

"I don't know what more you want. But if you mean he's a bit of a rustic"—from her self-conscious air he gathered that this was the latest phrase—"I'll go along with that."

"That still doesn't tell me—"

"Well, he's been in films forever, of course. But lately he's been playing *John Sherman, Special Agent,* on that television series. You must have seen him."

Maitland didn't answer that directly. "I think I see what you mean," he said. "No smoking, no drinking, no sex."

Lynn nodded. "It's a family program, but the queer thing is he's frightfully popular with all sorts of people. There's a fan club, and it's practically all teen-agers, you know. To be fair, I don't think that gives them the right to say how he should live, but I can quite see he wouldn't want anyone to know about Cynthia."

"Or to go about saying he'd murdered her," said Maitland, thinking at the same time what Sir Nicholas's feelings would have been if he could have heard this single-minded approach.

"Of course not. That's why I said it," the girl pointed out. Trying to catch John Lund's eye again, Antony found that the young man was gazing at her with an odd . . . surely a fatuous expression.

"Tell me about Cynthia, then," he said. But he was aware as he spoke of a certain depression of spirit, for surely this was an unlooked for, an unnecessary complication. If Johnny was falling in love. . . .

"There isn't very much to tell. She was younger than I am, just twenty-two, and she was on the stage . . . small part stuff, but she was good enough to get there, if she'd been given time. And she thought Paul was utterly marvelous, of course."

"But you didn't . . . or rather, you don't," he corrected himself.

She said, as she had said before, "He isn't my type."

"I see."

"What does that mean? Are you going to help me?"

"If I can." He thought about that for a moment. "One way or another, as best I can."

"That means you still don't believe—"

"No, look here, Miss Edison, that isn't really fair," protested

Johnny in the background. "Give us a chance to look into the matter."

"Thank you, I know what *that* means."

"What, for instance?" asked Maitland, interested.

"Oh . . . well . . . that you'll do your best, I suppose. But not that you'll try to find out—"

"You must be prepared for the possibility that there is nothing to find. Or that we are too dull to find it . . . which amounts to the same thing."

"But you'll try?"

Maitland nodded. "I just don't want you to build any false hopes, that's all."

"I'm so glad Meg sent me to you," said Lynn, smiling at him warmly. Antony smiled back, but he did not feel at all inclined to echo the sentiment. And he turned the subject—rather neatly, he thought—the next time Sir Nicholas adverted to it.

That was on Friday, and he had no opportunity of speaking his mind to Meg until the following day. The Maitlands had their own quarters at the top of Sir Nicholas Harding's house in Kempenfeldt Square—an arrangement which nobody regarded as temporary any more—and when Antony and Jenny got in from shopping on Saturday morning there was a message from Meg. "Come to lunch, I've something to tell you." Delivered in an expressionless voice by Gibbs, Sir Nicholas's butler, the words seemed robbed of meaning. Something nice . . . something of interest . . . something actively unpleasant? Jenny tried to telephone when they got upstairs, but there was no reply. Knowing Meg, the invitation had been given at a moment's notice, and she had rushed out to get supplies.

When they arrived at the tiny flat in Bayswater, that hadn't seemed tiny at all until Roger went to live there, there was no doubt how Meg regarded her news. She was bubbling over with it. "Darlings, we've got a house!"

They followed her into the room that had been such a perfect setting for Meg Hamilton, though never in exactly the way its designer, who was well known in theatrical circles, had intended. Nothing was changed now, the contents of the bookcase were still as shabby (but one door stood slightly ajar, as though it had been closed by too impatient a hand), a casual arrangement of daffodils and narcissus brightened a dark corner (but the vase had been pushed alarmingly near the edge of the table to make room for a pile of records), the same water color still hung tranquilly over the fireplace (but no longer quite straight). Everything was just as it had been . . . except that, if you knew Roger Farrell, you wouldn't doubt for a moment that he was in residence.

There was no reason for doubt at the moment, anyway. He got up from the desk as they went in. "Have you come to rejoice with us?" he asked. "Sit down and I'll get you a drink."

Jenny sat down obediently in the corner opposite the window. Antony commandeered the hearth rug. "Make the most of it," Meg advised. "Lunch will be frightful; I didn't know Roger would be in, and it's all frozen anyway."

"Some people," said Roger, with his back to the room, "might take that for a snub."

"Some people might be right," Meg retorted. She sat down herself and smiled at Jenny. "I'm all excited," she said. She had first made her name in London as Lady Macbeth, but on looks alone no one would have cast her for the part.

"Tell us, then. Is it a house you've just seen, or do you mean you've actually bought it?"

"Roger owned it all the time. He—he foreclosed on somebody," said Meg, as though the idea pleased her.

"I might have done if I'd thought of it—is that right for you, Jenny?—instead of living for nearly four years in hideous discomfort in this hole-in-the-wall of Meg's."

"Well, you must admit, darling, it sounds more romantic that way."

"Much less prosaic than just waiting for the lease to run out," he acknowledged.

"Tell us about it," said Jenny again.

"It's in Chelsea—"

"—Beaton Street, just above Battersea Bridge—"

"—and there aren't very many rooms, but they're quite a good size—"

"—and we can always do something with the attics if we have to."

Roger was still on his feet while he took part in this chorus, sipping his drink and watching Jenny's face as she tasted her gin and tonic, perhaps to see if it was mixed to her satisfaction. But Antony was watching Meg, with the amusement that was never very far below the surface of his thoughts. She had really changed so very little . . . as slim as ever, and with her dark hair still twisted round her head in a long plait. She said now, looking up at him but without any change of tone, "I know you're hating me, darling, but you must have seen for yourself that Lynn oughtn't to be let out alone."

"On the contrary, she seemed to me a singularly self-possessed young woman."

"What a horrid way of putting it," said Meg, revolted by this frankness. "At least you'll admit she's in the most dreadful trouble."

"Of course she is . . . through her own fault," Maitland added, with intent to annoy. Roger began to grin.

"I don't see that at all," Meg argued. "What would you do if someone murdered your sister?"

"I haven't got one."

"Darling, I thought you looked on me—"

"In that case I should give him a medal."

"You're not in a very nice frame of mind, are you?" said Meg, outraged. Her voice had deepened in sympathy with her mood. "And it isn't right for you to laugh like that, Roger, when I'm being insulted."

"If I read the situation correctly—" said Farrell, looking from one of them to the other, and then at Jenny again. "What *is* the situation?" he asked.

"Meg, being afraid that we might starve to death, has been putting some work in my way."

"Not again!"

"Yes, but it's different this time, darling," Meg protested. "I mean, it's all quite straightforward. Just an action for libel."

"Lynn Edison. I see," said Roger, resigned. He was a sturdily built man, not quite as tall as Maitland, but very near him in age. He had blue eyes and sandy hair, straight and rather thick. A forceful personality. "Why is it so dreadful?"

"Because we haven't a case at all—"

"But, darling, that's just why I wanted you to look after it," said Meg reasonably.

"—and I've promised the wretched girl to look into this justification plea of hers. Now, I ask you, Meg, is it likely that Paul Granville murdered anybody?"

"I don't suppose murder ever seems likely," said Jenny, who had been sitting quietly, listening, as she so often did. "Until we know it has happened, of course."

"But we don't know!"

"Then that's the first thing, isn't it? If you were sure the girl . . . I can't remember her name—"

"Cynthia."

"Yes, well, if you were sure she'd been murdered you could go on from there."

"But it's quite impossible to be sure of anything. If someone other than herself dissolved half a bottle of *Drowse* tablets in her coffee I don't suppose he did it before witnesses."

"It might be possible to create so strong a presumption of murder—" said Roger.

"How?"

"I don't know. Why did they say it was suicide? It's more customary to settle for an accident, if there's any doubt at all."

"Because one thing Lynn told me was correct," Maitland explained patiently. "Her sister had a horror of drugs of any kind, wouldn't have them in the house."

"In any case," said Meg, airily and inaccurately, "that's quite irrelevant. Why should she have killed herself, a girl like that?"

"That's what I've been wanting to ask you," Antony told her. "Like what?"

"Well . . . young, pretty, successful—"

"Yes, but was she?"

"Considering her age, quite successful. And going to be more so, I shouldn't wonder, as time went on."

"That's what Lynn said."

"She seems to me to have talked a great deal of sense," said Meg severely.

"Are you telling me *you* think Paul Granville—"

"I didn't say that."

"Go on talking about Cynthia, then. Was she working at the time of her death?"

"No, but she had been. *I Cannot Tell a Lie* had quite a long run. She was hoping for a part in *The Silent City*, I think . . . a big one."

"Her private life, then."

"She had lots of friends."

"Paul Granville among them?"

"I've heard . . . I don't know."

"That he was keeping her?"

"Well . . . yes."

"I don't care how much you hate gossip, Meg. You got me into this, and I've got to know—"

"They'd been together for six months or more," said Meg, still unwillingly. "Anyone would tell you . . . not just me."

"No secret about it?"

"None at all."

"That's something Lynn was wrong about then," he said, not without satisfaction.

"I don't suppose anybody would talk about it in front of her."

"Perhaps not. Any talk of the affair ending, or was it still in full swing?"

"As far as I know. I might not know, darling."

"Any more strings to her bow?"

There was a pause while Meg expressed her opinion, silently, of this vulgarity. "There's a man called William Anketell. He's producing *The Silent City,* as a matter of fact."

"No difficulty about her part, then?"

"That isn't what's being *said*."

"I suppose you're trying to tell me that he likes her, but she hasn't shown any sign of liking him."

"Something like that."

"And unless she did . . . all right, Meg, don't look so prim. Now you can tell me about Lynn Edison."

"She's a nice girl."

"Come now, *darling,* you can do better than that."

"Haven't you seen her program?" asked Roger, coming to life.

"You know we've managed to live so far without television."

"Yes, but . . . someone might have tried to educate you. I might have done so myself, if it had occurred to me. She's worth listening to, that girl."

"She said 'a commentary.' What sort of a commentary, anyway?"

"Anything and everything."

"Anything that's in the news," said Jenny, seeing that Antony was about to protest again at this vagueness. "It might be something really important, it might be something quite trivial—"

"She has a knack of stating the obvious," said Meg. "Only it isn't obvious until she says it, if you know what I mean."

"Near enough, I expect. She also had a job on the *Courier*—"

"Yes, but that's all I know about that."

"You sounded a moment ago as if you knew her quite well."

"I've met her everywhere," said Meg, with a comprehensive gesture that nearly spilled Jenny's drink. "At parties, you know. Tom Thorne used to bring her."

"Who is Tom Thorne?"

"He's the *Courier*'s drama critic, everyone knows that."

"Paul Granville then . . . what about him?"

"But you know—"

"He used to be in films, and now he's in a television series," said Maitland patiently. Then he smiled. "Lynn said he was 'a bit of a rustic.' What do you suppose she meant?"

"Well . . . a bit of a cad . . . a bounder," said Meg, searching her memory for the *mot juste*. "And I must say that comes very well from her."

"What do you mean?"

"She used to like him . . . I've heard she did," Meg corrected herself.

"I don't like the sound of that." Antony exchanged a look with Roger, and saw that the statement had struck him the same way. "Hell hath no fury, and all that sort of thing. How many people do you suppose will be prepared to go into the witness box and swear to that?"

"I don't know." Meg was worried now, and showed it. "I hadn't thought of it in that way but"—she spread her hands again—"everyone said it."

"Well, perhaps it won't occur to anyone to repeat it in court."

"Can you do anything, Antony? Anything at all?"

"I rather doubt it. I think she's sincere, you know, but I think she's wrong."

"Then what will happen? To Lynn?"

"The jury will find for the plaintiff, and if he's as popular as everyone says he is the damages will be pretty heavy. She'll be left without a penny, and without much hope of getting a job. I don't like the idea any more than you do, Meg, but I don't see what we can do about it now."

"What will she do?"

"She says she can type. Not much fun, I should think."

"But the real thing is what people will think," said Meg tragically.

"What do they think now?"

"Well, it's exciting. Rather fun to think he *might* have done it. But once the case is over—"

"You're right, of course. They'll turn on her to a man."

"To a woman, darling. I like Lynn. I think you ought to do something to stop her spoiling her life."

"What, for instance?"

"Can't you explain that she didn't know what she was saying?"

"Only with her consent. I'm hoping that when she's had time to think over what I told her—to worry about it, I suppose I should say—I may be able to persuade her—" But Meg came to her feet before he had finished speaking, uttered a piercing scream, and rushed away to save her luncheon from—she said when she returned—utter annihilation.

The meal was, predictably, much better than she had forecast. The talk went back to the house again, and its possibilities, and Meg became quite starry-eyed . . . according to Roger at the thought of spending money. It wasn't until they had left the table and were sitting over coffee that Farrell returned, unexpectedly, to the subject of Paul Granville.

"I can tell you one thing that isn't generally known about him," he said. "He's a gambler."

"What sort?"

"I've seen him at the *Hazard Club*. The play's pretty high there."

"Is that how you spend your spare time, darling?" Meg inquired plaintively.

"I went with a client. I think it was his idea of showing his gratitude for a tip I gave him," said Farrell, who was a stockbroker. "I have to do something while you're at the theater," he pointed out. But you needn't worry, I have no sporting blood."

"I thought your whole life was one continual gamble," said Antony reflectively. "Perhaps you get it out of your system that way."

"Perhaps I do."

"What was Granville playing?"

"Nothing, when I saw him. Just walking around, observing human nature."

"That doesn't mean anything, darling," said Meg, dividing the endearment between them. "He owns the *Hazard Club*."

"I didn't know that." Roger was immediately interested.

"There must be money in his particular brand of soothing syrup, I suppose."

"Enough to get started on. He rented the house at first, but somebody told me he'd bought it outright since then."

"How do you know all this?"

"But, darling, it's common knowledge." She glanced at Roger, and smiled at him. "If I'd known you'd be interested I'd have told you before."

"Well, I'm glad to know it, of course," said Maitland, following single-mindedly his own train of thought. "But I don't see how it helps me, do you?"

Roger didn't. Nor did Meg. Nor did Jenny, though she returned to the subject when they were on their way home. "I think you ought to be careful, Antony."

"How do you mean?"

She thought about that for a moment. "I don't like Paul Granville. He has a mean mouth."

This was so unlike Jenny that he turned to look at her. She was sitting perfectly relaxed, as always when she was driving, and she smiled when she felt his eyes on her, but did not take her own from the road. "If he really did murder that girl—"

"Jenny love, my inquiries will be discretion itself."

And of course he meant it. And of course they were. But he had to admit, later, that discretion isn't always enough.

heard the broadcast they thought—of course!—that she knew something."

"Do they all say that? Separately, or in chorus?"

"Variations on a theme. I've got the statements here if you want to see them," said Johnny, reaching down to pat the brief case beside his chair, rather as if it was a dog that sat there, so that Maitland was moved to protest.

"Not more paper. Not until you've told me—"

"That's all. Isn't it enough? Except Granville himself, of course."

"And what will Granville say?"

"That he was keeping Cynthia Edison, though they each maintained a separate establishment," said Johnny, with scorn in his voice for a stilted phrase. "He must know we could prove that bit."

"Or perhaps he has a passion for honesty."

"Perhaps. He will also say she was of a mercurial temperament—do you suppose he really talks like this?"

"I should consider it unlikely."

"I don't know why they can't report him accurately then. She was of a mercurial temperament," said Johnny, who had obviously learned this bit by heart, "and though he had never considered the possibility of her committing suicide he couldn't say he was altogether surprised when she did."

"What does Lynn have to say about that?"

"All lies."

"And the three friends? Or didn't they know Cynthia?"

"They corroborate Granville's statement on all points."

"Do they though? I wonder if we couldn't, just possibly, shake them a little."

Johnny grinned. "I expect you could, but it doesn't really help to prove Paul Granville is a murderer."

"How true! The more I think about this business, Johnny, the more I think we can best serve Lynn Edison by enlisting the court's sympathy on her behalf."

WEDNESDAY, 7th February

I

Johnny Lund arrived in chambers with a bulging brief case and a harassed look. "I've been working on it," he said, spreading papers across Maitland's desk with a lavish hand, "but I don't seem to get anywhere."

"What have you got?" asked Antony, averting his eyes, and taking an envelope out of his pocket to make notes on. He could think of nothing he wished to do less at the moment than to plow through the mass of documents that Johnny seemed determined to unload on him.

"Their case," said Lund briskly. "Three chaps who were monitoring the program. They probably won't use them all when they know we're not disputing the fact. Head of the department that conducts listener surveys, to say how many people were likely, in his estimation, to hear the libel. Daniel Owen, to show how magnanimous Granville was prepared to be. Three other friends of Granville's to say that when they

23

"She won't like that."

"If I can help it she won't realize what we're doing."

"I see." Johnny sounded doubtful. "It seems to me you made her a promise—"

"To look into the question of Granville's guilt. So I did . . . and so I will. But I won't go into court with an accusation I don't believe in, and I can't say I'm very optimistic that anything will come of our inquiries."

"N-no."

"What do you think about that?"

"I want to do whatever's best for her, of course."

"Paul Granville also has his point of view."

"So he has, but it isn't up to us to consider it."

"Who's acting for him?"

"Halloran."

"We certainly don't need to worry about him in that case." But he looked thoughtful, and Johnny said uneasily,

"Is he good?"

"Very good indeed. What does Granville say he was doing *that* night?"

"The night Cynthia was poisoned?"

"January the fourteenth; it was a Sunday."

"He says he never went to Guildford Place at all that day."

"Could he have got in and out unobserved?"

"Quite easily. There's a caretaker, but not a doorman."

"We can assume, then, that if he did go nobody saw him," said Maitland, depressed by the thought.

"I'm afraid so. What he does say is that he was at home playing records. He lives alone in a service flat, so there seems to be no chance of proving or disproving that either."

"What was the state of his relationship with Cynthia Edison?"

"They were on excellent terms. He loved her as much as ever," said Johnny, quoting again, "and was heartbroken when he heard of her death."

"The last time he saw her—"

"Only the day before. She was a little quiet in her manner, but if he'd realized how depressed she was he'd have gone to her on the Sunday as well . . . of course."

"I'm beginning to dislike Mr. Granville. He has an answer for everything."

"He won't be easy to deal with in court either, being so well used to appearing in public." Johnny slipped easily into the role of Job's comforter.

"That had already occurred to me. Does he take *Drowse,* by the way, or know anyone who does?"

"He doesn't take it himself, and if any of his friends do he's not aware of the fact."

"Has he ever purchased it?"

"He says not."

"And who are we to disbelieve him? I shall want an account of the inquest, you know."

"If you'd look at what I've brought you—" Johnny's tone was faintly injured.

"There's so much of it," Maitland complained. "Anyway, you've had an opportunity to digest it, so you may as well tell me—"

"It all sounded fairly cut and dried. She was found by the cleaning woman when she went in at nine o'clock on the Monday morning."

"In bed?"

"No, still in the sitting room. The curtains were drawn, and the lights were on, and she was sitting on the sofa—"

"Not lying down?"

"I don't think so. There was a tray in front of her with a coffee pot and sugar basin, and one cup . . . a tea cup, not one of those fiddling little things. There was a magazine open on the cushion beside her—*Woman's Review*—and she'd been smoking, because there was a pile of stubs in the ashtray, all with her lipstick."

"Does Paul Granville smoke?"

"I don't know."

"Never mind. We've left the cleaning woman behind now, haven't we?"

"Yes. *Drowse* is in tablet form, but easily soluble in anything hot. It's put up in bottles of fifty or a hundred—this was the large size—and the doctor says she must have taken about twenty . . . considerably more than a fatal dose."

"Wouldn't it taste?"

"Apparently not, in black, sweetened coffee. That's what the doctor says, but the point didn't arise really, because no one seems to have queried suicide at all."

"How long would she take to die?"

"Quite some time. He was a bit vague about that. But she'd go into a coma within ten or fifteen minutes, after such a heavy dose."

"I see. What about the police evidence?"

"In general, no sign that she had had a visitor that evening. In particular, no suicide note, but she had a pad and pencil on the tray so they think she must have meant to write one and been overcome before she could do so. As for the coffee, if the pot had been full she'd drunk three cups of it. The *Drowse* had been dissolved in the cup, not in the pot."

"The bottle?"

"On the tray, empty. A blur of fingerprints, and Cynthia's on top of the rest. Two of her friends swore she'd never have so much as an aspirin in the house, and the cleaning woman confirmed it. That's all really."

"Not quite. Something must have been said about her state of mind."

"Not much. She was resting. She was anxious about her next part. An apparent absence of motive on her part isn't really enough to base an accusation of murder on, you know," said Johnny seriously.

"It isn't, is it?" Maitland agreed, amused. It occurred to him that Johnny, with the earnestness of youth, probably considered him incurably light-minded. "Have you thought at all about the order in which we should present our case?"

"We haven't got one."

"No, I mean, whether we should make a push to have the last word in court."

"You've been looking up precedents too."

"For my sins." He turned over the envelope on which he had been writing and scowled down at the words he had scrawled there. "Cooper *versus* Wakley (1828) . . . would that be what you mean?"

"It would. Justification was the only issue there and the defendant was given the right to open the case and call his witnesses first. I can't make up my mind if it would be a good thing, or not."

"Well, we needn't decide just yet. What about these friends of Cynthia's? And the cleaning woman."

"I've got their addresses."

"And that chap Anketell?"

"I've made an appointment for tomorrow morning at his office."

"Good. It will be a start, anyway." He hesitated. "Or rather, I'm making a start this evening . . . in a way. Roger Farrell is taking me to the *Hazard Club*."

"What has that to do with all this?"

"Nothing, so far as I know. Granville owns it, that's all."

"I don't see—"

"Neither do I. If I'm lucky I shall get a sight of the gentleman, completely unofficially. I cannot conceive," he added, with a momentary, unconscious echo of Sir Nicholas's manner, "that it will do me the slightest good."

"Do you want me? I expect I could arrange—"

"Unofficially, I said, Johnny. No need for your presence at all."

"That's good!" His tone was too hearty, and he went on self-consciously, "I only mean, I'm taking Lynn Edison out to dinner."

"Enjoy yourselves."

"I expect we shall." Johnny paused, and looked rather searchingly at his companion. "What's on your mind?"

"Only that . . . she's a client. It makes things awkward, don't you think?"

"It needn't. Our relationship is as correct as you please. I don't even know whether . . . well, whether there's anybody else."

Which all goes to show, thought Maitland, vaguely comforted, that we all take refuge in banalities in times of stress. Jenny, however, was quite definitely in disagreement with his attitude when he told her about the conversation that night.

"I hope you didn't say anything to put him off, Antony. It's high time he settled down."

"But . . . Lynn Edison?"

"I thought she sounded nice."

"From what I told you?"

"Yes."

"Jenny love, your imagination's working overtime."

"You'd like her yourself if you'd stop thinking of her as a—a problem."

"How can I? And that goes for Johnny, too. He has enough troubles of his own over this case, without taking on hers as well."

"A trouble shared—" said Jenny, and laughed as she spoke, but her gray eyes were serious. And then Roger arrived, and Antony forgot the subject again, though it remained, a small added uneasiness, at the back of his mind.

II

The *Hazard Club* occupied a tall house in Bourdon Lane, which is narrow enough to discourage traffic. They paid off the taxi at the corner, where a building was being demolished; to make room for another block of flats, according to the signboard. There were a few pedestrians about, but they all seemed to be imbued with a sense of purpose. The three men went along the street until they reached the club, which, viewed from the outside, was deceptively quiet.

Roger's client, who was sponsoring them, was a pleasant, incurious individual, and disappeared into the crowd almost as soon as the formalities were complete. Maitland lingered to admire the fine proportions of the hall in which they stood, before he followed Roger into the first salon, which was full of light and noise, and over-full of people. The decorations, so far as in the circumstances they could be observed, seemed to be all in period. . . . Regency, he thought vaguely. There could be little doubt that money had been spent on the furnishing of the house, as well as on the fabric, but looking at the crowd it seemed likely that there was a fair return on whatever investment had been involved.

They paused by one of the tables; there seemed to be as many spectators as players here. Antony heard a woman beside him catch her breath, and then release it in a long sigh; the *croupier* sounded bored, world-weary; a man elbowed past him to lay a last minute bet; the wheel spun. "Nothing to see here," said Roger inaccurately. "Let's go into the smaller salon. Come on."

Again Maitland followed, threading his way with some difficulty. In the room beyond it was different; here the game was quiet, perhaps more deadly, and the only light shone down directly on the table, leaving the corners of the room in shadow. "Baccarat," said Roger softly, to his friend. And then, "What do you think of them?"

"I think—" They were intent, so intent upon the turn of the cards that it was frightening. The distinguished-looking man who might have been an ambassador; the little, dark, ugly man, who might have been a jockey from his size, the girl whose hair shone softly gold when she leaned forward into the circle of lamplight, so that he thought for a moment, incongruously, of Jenny; the older woman, beautifully groomed, whose eyes held an almost feverish anxiety; what was the lure that attracted them, that kept them here, enthralled, hour upon hour? "I don't like the smell of the place," said Antony decidedly; but he, too, spoke in a low voice.

"You wanted to come."

"Of course I did. I've got to come somehow to an understanding of Paul Granville."

"And you think this will help you?"

"It might. Is he here?" He was looking about him as he spoke.

"I haven't seen him. Perhaps in the mob back there—"

"Heaven forbid."

"—perhaps in the supper room. Shall we go and see?"

"I could do with a drink."

They began to make their way toward the doorway. Maitland was moving a little stiffly, a fact that Roger observed, but did not comment on. It meant that he was tired, or that his shoulder was paining him. "There's someone I know," said Farrell, as they stepped into the hall. "Danny Owen."

"I don't . . . oh, yes, I remember, Granville's agent."

"That's right." Roger raised a hand in salutation, and a sandy-haired man, short and rather thickly built, responded with a wave and disappeared into the main salon.

"I don't want to meet him," said Antony, "but I wonder what he's doing here."

"Perhaps his activities extend to every aspect of Granville's affairs."

"Perhaps they do."

He sounded pleased, and Roger asked curiously, "I don't see how that helps you," his tone making the words a question.

"Come now, it may be very helpful indeed."

"In court?"

"Precisely."

"Well, I don't . . . oh, hallo, Whitehead," he added, as a tall, bald man came up to them, beaming.

"Fancy seeing you here, Mr. Farrell, after all this time."

"Let me introduce—"

"Oscar Whitehead," said the newcomer, shaking Antony enthusiastically by the hand.

"—Antony Maitland."

The shaggy eyebrows gave character to Whitehead's face, which otherwise was smooth and bland. Beneath them his eyes were bright and curious. "Maitland," he repeated. "I seem to have heard your name."

"You'll find it in the history books," said Antony, taking refuge in garrulousness because he had no wish to explain himself. "A rather sinister character, I always thought. Or there was a Captain Maitland who escorted Napoleon to Elba; perhaps you were thinking of him."

"No . . . no . . . I shall have it in a minute. Something to do with the law."

"I'm a barrister," said Maitland, seeing there was no help for it.

"Well, I admit, I don't rightly understand your arrangements over here." Even without the implication of this, Antony thought, there was no mistaking his transatlantic origin. "But you're interested," said Whitehead, interrupting himself, "in all this."

"Very interested indeed. Is there always such a crowd?"

"At this time of night, yes, usually. Things begin to liven up at about eleven o'clock."

"What's your game, Mr. Whitehead?"

"Baccarat, when I play at all. I guess I'm more of an onlooker really. But in general you can take it that everyone who comes here as a visitor has a go . . . sooner or later."

"I see. Are you concerned with the management then?"

"I take an interest . . . sure I do. It's my business, in a way, back home."

"A nostalgic interest. But I hope you're having a pleasant trip," said Antony politely.

"It's always a pleasure to stay in your beautiful country." That was politeness, too; the day had been cold and blustery, no pleasure to anyone. "A long visit this time, however." His eyes flickered momentarily to rest on Roger's face. "I've been here almost a year."

"Observing?" said Maitland idly, and was startled to receive, in return for the question, a look that was very far from casual. But Whitehead's voice was as smooth as ever when he replied.

"You could call it that. I'm always ready to learn, and I just naturally take notice of my surroundings, I guess."

"This place, now . . . would you say it was a paying proposition?" He thought he knew the answer to that already; the *Hazard Club* smelled of success.

Whitehead looked amused. "The law's a queer thing over here," he said. "Talk about giving with one hand and taking away with the other. But you'd know more about that than I do, I expect."

"Not my line of country, I'm afraid."

"Well, first they made gambling legal, and then they tied it up with all these restrictions. Take roulette, for instance, will you believe me that the house has no advantage, percentagewise, over the player."

"Hasn't it?" said Maitland, rather blankly.

"It's really quite simple . . . but unprofitable, of course."

"Why do they still keep it going then?"

"They're hoping to appeal the decision," said Roger, coming back into the conversation. It still startled Antony from time to time that so energetic an individual should be able, when he wished, to efface himself so completely. "Meanwhile, it's a matter of keeping their clients' goodwill . . . and their licenses, I suppose."

"Even so—"

"There are ways of circumventing the law. If you try your hand at roulette, for instance, and if you win—"

"Do you think I might?" said Antony hopefully.

"No, I don't. *If* you win, in addition to the regular payoff, you'll be paid the zero or house percentage in plastic chips."

"The wheels on this side of the water have a single zero, which gives the house an edge of two point seven percent over the player," said Whitehead helpfully, which only added to Maitland's confusion.

"That's all very well," he said, "but how does it get around the difficulty? I should be playing with chips anyway, shouldn't I?"

"Yes, but these are different. Distinctive. The idea is, you see, that you shouldn't cash them in, thus allowing the house a fair profit. A sort of gentleman's agreement . . . or would be if they didn't have to stress its voluntary nature."

"And this—this *ex gratia* payment keeps on the right side of the law?"

"That's the beauty of it . . . nobody knows."

"There is still the baccarat table," Whitehead reminded them.

"All the same, it sounds pretty dicey to me."

"You're thinking of craps, Mr. Maitland. Baccarat is—" He broke off and smiled from one of them to the other. "There I go, taking you literally. But why are you so interested in all this? Are you going to play, or are you thinking of making an investment?"

"I doubt if I could afford either. Just my insatiable curiosity, I'm afraid."

"It isn't always wise to be too curious." This was said lightly, his smile broadened as he spoke. "You always run the risk of being disillusioned."

There was a pause. "We're going to have a drink," said Roger into the silence. "Won't you join us?"

"Not just now. I'm going to take a look at the play, and maybe find a place at the baccarat table." He turned away as he spoke, and a moment later Maitland saw him in the doorway of the main salon, in apparently earnest consultation with Danny Owen who was on his way out. He did not see Oscar Whitehead again during the hour they spent between the supper room and the salons.

He did get a look at Paul Granville, however, studying the actor covertly as he stood in talk with a group of men and women . . . the ambassador, who had evidently wearied of bac-

34

carat, or perhaps his luck was out; a tall, wonderfully elegant woman in a red dress; a little, dark, eager woman; a man in a gray suit that looked as if it might have been slept in. Granville himself was older than he had appeared in the film . . . in his late thirties perhaps. A handsome man who somehow conveyed the impression that he was only too conscious of his charm. Or was that a fair judgment? No lack of intelligence, at least. A worthy adversary. But was that fair either? Could the man stand there so calmly self-possessed if somewhere in the background of his thought there lay the memory of Cynthia Edison's murder? The answer to that was, of course, that he could, very easily. But what reason was there to believe it, after all? Lynn Edison's reiterated statement didn't amount to proof.

Farrell was patient enough with Maitland's delays, but he was yawning by the time they came down the steps into the street. The wind was as cold as ever, and there was a dampness in the air, as though it might be going to snow. "If you'd wanted to play I could have understood it," he said.

"Didn't you think it was interesting? I did."

"I could see that. But what did you learn that you didn't know already?"

"One thing, at least. Those people"—he jerked his head as he spoke—"are caught just as surely as if someone were feeding them drugs."

"That doesn't make Granville a murderer."

"No," Maitland agreed. They walked for a few moments in silence. "Tell me about your friend Whitehead."

"I only met him once. He's a friend of Carpenter's, and stayed with us for most of the evening."

"Was he playing?"

"No."

"He warned me off the grass neatly . . . don't you think?"

"You were being damned rude," said Roger bluntly. They were walking under the scaffolding now, where the demolition was taking place.

"Not in the best of taste, perhaps. But not actually rude un-

35

less it was his own affairs I was questioning, and if you noticed, he was vague about that."

"You've got some idea in your head," said Roger in a resigned tone. "I might have known it, I suppose."

"Only that I think he has more to do with the *Hazard Club* than he wants us to know."

"How do you make that out?"

"Actions and reactions. We may as well find a cab, you can drop me on your way." They reached the corner as he spoke, and paused under the street lamp, looking around them. And the next instant Roger had grabbed Antony's arm and dragged him sideways. There was a moment of sickening pain as something struck his right shoulder, and then he was staring down at a jagged lump of masonry which had come to rest in the precise spot where he had been standing.

III

Jenny disconcerted him by being awake when he got home, and because he couldn't hope to hide the bandage in which Dr. Prescott had insisted on swathing him he told her more or less what had happened after they left the club. Jenny sat up in bed, hugging her knees. "Antony, are you sure it was an accident?"

She had an awkward habit of phrasing her questions so that the only reply was the truth, or the lie direct; which, though he was quite ready to indulge in evasive tactics, he had an odd scruple about using. "Of course I'm not sure," he said, with a trace of irritation in his voice. And then, seeing that she was still eyeing him accusingly, "Oh, well, I suppose I'd better tell you. I'm sure it wasn't."

"I told you something dreadful would happen—"

"It wasn't dreadful. Roger's reactions are much quicker than mine. And if it hadn't been my right shoulder there'd have been very little harm done."

"You might have been killed."

"Well, I wasn't. Don't keep on about it, love."

"What did the doctor say?"

" 'Whatever happened, I expect it was your own fault.' "

Jenny smiled at the mimicry, but not as if her heart was in it. "That wasn't what I meant."

"It'll be all right in a couple of days. Don't worry so."

"I don't honestly see how I can help it. You sounded very sure, Antony. How did you know?"

"That it wasn't an accident? Unless the law of gravity was temporarily suspended—"

"I don't understand at all. It didn't come up and hit you."

"No, but to clear the scaffolding it must have been tossed. Roger saw that at once. And that being so, it was the merest chance it hit me at all."

"Someone must have thought it was worth their while to try."

"I know what you're thinking, but can you really see Paul Granville climbing about on a half-demolished building?"

"One of his employees at the club—" She broke off to consider the suggestion. "It would be an awfully difficult thing to ask anyone to do for you, wouldn't it?"

"Embarrassing," Antony agreed. His annoyance had faded now, to be replaced by a more characteristic, if rather wry amusement. "It was a half-hearted business, after all. As for who was responsible, who lives may learn."

But it cannot be said that either of them slept very well for what remained of the night.

THURSDAY, *8th February*

I

Maitland thought he knew perfectly well what the office of a theatrical producer would be like, and of course the reality was quite different from his imagining. For that matter, William Anketell didn't come up to specification either . . . a large, shabby man in a large, shabby office. His secretary, however, might have been type-cast for the part . . . a glamour girl with a formidable air of efficiency. She kept Antony waiting for ten minutes before summoning him, and provided only the *Courier*, which he had already seen, by way of solace. He reread the headlines . . . FRESH MOVES IN MIDDLE EAST CRISIS . . . . BANK CASHIER SHOT IN DARING RAID . . . . CABINET MINISTER HINTS AT RESIGNATION . . . . and was glad when she intimated graciously that his vigil was over.

Anketell offered cigarettes, and produced a pipe for himself, which he proceeded to fill with slow, measured movements. "I'm not quite sure what I can do for you," he said.

For that matter, Antony didn't feel too clear about it himself. "I need to talk to some of Cynthia Edison's friends."

"It's this business of the libel action, isn't it? Don't tell me you're taking Lynn seriously."

"Shouldn't I?"

"Of course not. She's a clever girl, mind, but she has some scatty ideas."

"Do you know her well?"

"Not so well as I knew Cynthia." He paused, puffing on the pipe; as far as Antony could tell, he felt no emotion at all. "That's why you're here, I suppose."

"I hoped you might tell me—"

"I wanted to marry her, you know." Anketell was pursuing his own train of thought. "If she hadn't been so taken up with Paul . . . but that's not to say he killed her." He looked across at his visitor through a wreath of smoke. "I wish I agreed with Lynn about that, but I don't."

"Why do you wish—?"

"Not just because I was jealous of him. Not only that. Something happened to make her want to die."

"And you think it was connected with Paul Granville?"

"What else can I think? Look here, what have you heard about Cynthia?"

"She was an actress," said Maitland carefully, "and her temperament was mercurial."

"She was an actress, and a good one too. As for what she was like,"—and now there was all the emotion that had seemed lacking before, naked in his eyes—"she was happy, and sweet-tempered, and lovely to look at. Not morbid at all."

"When did you last see her?"

"The Friday before she died." He pulled a desk diary toward him, and flipped over the pages. "The twelfth of January, that would be."

"Here, in your office?"

"Where else? As far as she was concerned, she was married to Paul. She'd have considered anything else disloyal."

"I see. So it was purely a business meeting?"

"Haven't I said so? I was casting *The Silent City* and I wanted her to take the lead."

"You wanted her . . . did she know?"

"It was hardly a thing I'd have kept a secret from her. Yes, she knew."

"That was quite a step forward in her career, wasn't it? Was she pleased?"

"Ecstatic . . . I thought."

"But then—"

"That's why I said it must have been something in her personal life."

"Something that happened between the time she left you . . . when was that?"

"About four o'clock. She wanted to get home before Paul arrived, she said."

"Do you think—I'm sorry to have to ask you this—do you think she was a suicidal type?"

"Is there such a thing? I've already made it clear—"

"You said she wasn't morbid. But still you think she killed herself, don't you?"

"What else can I think? I was at the inquest and those two girls—Irene Brooke and Harriet something-or-other—they were quite right in what they said. At least, I've known her to have a violent headache and refuse to take anything for it. So I don't imagine she kept any drugs in the house."

"That rules out accident, unless she changed her mind," said Maitland thoughtfully. "What do you think happened, Mr. Anketell?"

"They might have had a row, or he might have grown tired of her and wanted to end the association. Could Lynn get away with it on those grounds . . . that she meant he was morally responsible?"

That was a question he didn't want to answer. Not now, not to Anketell. "You say you know her. She's a very determined person . . . don't you think?"

"I'm afraid I agree with you. I wish she hadn't stirred up all this, you know, but as she has . . . I wish she had half a chance of getting away with it."

"You can't tell me anything else about Cynthia's relationship with Paul Granville?"

"Nothing at all . . . except that I hated it."

"She didn't say anything, that last afternoon?"

"Nothing but what I told you. We talked about the play, she seemed happy and excited, just how I'd have expected her to be. We . . . but that was all that mattered."

"Are you sure?"

"It can't help you to know I asked her again to marry me. I knew what the answer would be. So then she said Paul was recording, and would get to Guildford Place about four-thirty. She left in time to get there first."

"There was nothing . . . well, nothing suggestive of an emotional upset in the way she spoke?"

"Nothing at all." The pipe had gone out; he reached absent-mindedly for a box of matches. "Nothing that I noticed at the time."

"Afterward?"

"Oh . . . afterward. I thought she seemed nervous. . . . I thought she seemed unhappy. . . . I tried to persuade myself that one of those things was true. Because I hated Paul, you see, and I wanted his conscience to reproach him, if nothing else. If he has one, of course."

"Do you think I shall find Miss Brooke—did you say?—and the other girl reliable witnesses?"

"I don't know anything about them really. They were right about one thing . . . I told you that."

"Yes . . . well . . . I'm very grateful to you, Mr. Anketell. If I want to see you again—"

"I shall be only too glad." But he came to his feet as he spoke, and now it seemed he was urgent for the visitor to be gone.

Detective Chief Inspector Sykes of the C.I.D. was a placid man, but persistent. His third phone call coincided with Maitland's arrival in chambers just before noon. "If you've an hour or so to spare," he suggested, "we might have lunch together."

"That sounds a good idea."

"At Brackett's, then. Shall we say one o'clock."

"Whenever you like, Chief Inspector." But he was looking thoughtful as he replaced the receiver.

It was pleasantly warm, coming into the restaurant from the wind-swept street. Sykes was already installed in his favorite corner. He was a square-built, fresh-faced man, rather heavy about the jaw, and his tweeds might easily have suggested the farmer had not his look of rather benevolent complacency put that idea out of court. He greeted Antony now with every evidence of pleasure, and inquired punctiliously after Jenny's health and Sir Nicholas's before coming to the point.

"As for you, Mr. Maitland, I'm sorry to hear you've been in the wars again."

"Now, how did you know that?" He wasn't wearing the sling the doctor had recommended, and though his shoulder was rather more painful than usual he didn't realize how much the stiffness of his movements might betray to an observant eye.

"A man giving your name was hit by a piece of falling masonry last night in Waverton Square. He disclaimed any intention of suing, but people have been known to change their minds, and the constable on the beat took down what particulars he could."

"I know all that. You needn't be so cautious."

"You'd be surprised how things get about, Mr. Maitland, you really would."

"All right, I am surprised. What about it?"

"Were you badly hurt? The constable thought—"

"It was nothing," said Antony rather abruptly. He sat back to let the waiter serve his soup, and did not say anything more until they were alone again. "You still haven't told me what this is about."

"You'd been visiting the *Hazard Club*," said Sykes, picking up his spoon.

"Don't tell me you want to warn me of the evils of gambling. I've done plenty of silly things in my time, but that isn't one of them."

"No. I was just wondering—knowing you as I do, Mr. Maitland—whether what happened was an accident or not."

"I suppose you think it's a natural, human instinct to throw bricks at me on sight." He was eating soup, clumsily, with his left hand, but he looked up to smile at the detective.

"I should hardly go as far as that," said Sykes reflectively. "But you haven't answered my question, you know."

"I know." He thought about it for a moment. "It wasn't an accident," he said.

"Are you sure about that?"

"It had to be thrown, to clear the scaffolding. Very much a hit or miss affair."

"Somebody who hoped to injure you, but didn't mind if you were killed in the process."

"That follows, doesn't it?" There was a pause, while they both concentrated on their soup. "We're taking a good deal for granted, aren't we? It might have been Roger Farrell they were out to get."

"Knowing you—"

"Yes, Chief Inspector, you needn't spell it out for me. It is much more likely that I was the intended victim. And now I suppose you want to know why."

"Of course."

"I don't know."

"I'm sure you have some idea—"

"Oh, ideas! Nothing you'd be interested in, I'm afraid."

"What were you doing at the *Hazard Club,* if you didn't go there to play?"

"Observing."

"Why there particularly?"

"Because it belongs to Paul Granville, and I'm acting for Miss Lynn Edison, who is being sued for libel."

"That's something I didn't know, Mr. Maitland. That you were representing her, I mean."

"I'm glad to learn you aren't completely omniscient. And I'm not trying to imply that Granville had anything to do with what happened. I should think it was most unlikely."

"Who then?"

"Someone who knew I'd gone to the club, and was on the lookout for me leaving. The lighting is good on the corner, there's a street lamp there, and we had a quick look around afterward; it didn't need an acrobat to do the climb. I'd say it was someone from the club if that didn't seem so senseless. . . . I mean, it would have been a dead giveaway that they had something to hide."

"We aren't getting anywhere, are we, Mr. Maitland?"

"As far as I'm concerned, there's nowhere to get. What do you know about the Betting and Gaming Act?"

"A worse day's work the Government never did," said Sykes heavily.

"I daresay. I've been looking it up this morning, and it seems a bit complicated to me."

"I thought that was done on purpose, to make work for the lawyers," said Sykes innocently.

Maitland grinned, but otherwise ignored the shaft. "The gaming must be so conducted that the chances are equally favorable to all the players," he said. "There's also a bit about no stake money being applied except as payment of winnings, but it's the first rule that seems important."

"Important, in what way?"

"In deciding whether a club is profitable to operate or not."

"It's not very long since the final decision was reached in a trial case that went as far as the Lords. After that it was quite clear they had to operate without using the zero, and that—so far as I know—is what most of them are doing."

"Yes, but are they running at a profit now?"

"That's something else again. There are other games played too, besides roulette. Then again, I understand there's a move on foot to get the law revised, and they're hopeful of a happy result . . . for them."

"Do you think they'll succeed?"

"As to that, we haven't shot our bolt ourselves yet. The position is by no means finally clarified."

"I see." There was an interval while their soup plates were removed, and steak and kidney pie—recommended by Sykes as a speciality of the house—substituted. "Why did you say 'a worse day's work?' " asked Maitland, between mouthfuls.

"Because it opened the way to all sorts of abuses."

"The Lords' decision ought to help matters."

"Make them worse more like," said Sykes gloomily. "If they can't get their profits legally—"

"I understood they had ways and means of getting around the law."

"Temporarily, perhaps. It can't last. And that's what I wanted to speak to you about, Mr. Maitland. Not that I suppose it will do the slightest good."

"I don't quite see—"

"I don't want to see you getting out of your depth."

"You *are* afraid I'm bound for hell by the shortest road, aren't you?"

"No. No, nothing like that. But we're getting a lot of bad characters in from the continent and from America. They're using the respectable houses as a front . . . where a chap's glad of some extra capital, for instance, and doesn't realize where it's leading him. Then they set up their own rackets . . . protection, narcotics, the numbers game—"

"I've always wondered what that was."

"A sort of lottery." Sykes brushed the interruption impatiently aside. "They're showing signs of organizing our criminals, too. The idea, of course, is that we're not set up to deal

45

with that sort of thing, so they're making hay while the sun shines. I'm warning you, don't tangle with them, that's all."

"Chief Inspector, I've never seen you so worked up."

"Have you listened to one word of what I was saying?" said Sykes, exasperated.

"To every word. Can you doubt it? The thing is, I'm interested in the gambling setup, but it's really none of my business."

"Then the sooner you manage to convey that fact to the persons concerned the better."

"Yes, but who are they?"

There was a pause before Sykes answered him, and then what he had to say seemed irrelevant. "You said you had a quick look around on the demolition site, but there was one thing you missed."

"What was that?"

"A man had been shot. I'm not surprised you didn't see him; the body had been dragged out of sight behind a pile of bricks."

"But—" said Antony, and stopped. "That makes the whole thing even more senseless," he said. And then, "Who was it, do you know?"

"A young chap called Eddie Baker."

"Never heard of him."

"Are you sure?"

"Of course I'm sure. If that's his own name."

"He's well known to the police. I never heard of him using an alias."

"Tell me about him then."

"Petty criminal, easily resorts to violence. I'm slandering him at that; we've never managed to get him inside. A bit trigger happy, you might say, if that didn't seem to imply that he specialized in firearms, which he didn't."

"Well, I don't see . . . when was he found?"

"This morning when the first workmen arrived."

"Then he might have been shot after we left the area, or hours before."

"It's like this, Mr. Maitland: from the position of the blood-stains it looked as if he'd been climbing down the inside of the building—after his attempt on your life, it might be—when someone came up close behind him and shot him in the back."

"I see."

"Did you hear anything?"

"We wouldn't have done if a silencer was used. There was still quite a bit of traffic about. And we were talking to the constable for a while—at least Roger was. There'd have been plenty of time. The only thing is, whichever way you look at it, it doesn't make sense."

"What were you doing at the *Hazard Club* last night?"

"I told you . . . observing. And that reminds me, I met a man called Whitehead."

"What about him?"

"He's an American, and he runs, or ran, a gaming house 'back home.' "

"There, you see!"

"What do I see?"

"Not that I wouldn't rather he'd had one of these fancy, Italian names. They most of them have."

"You're hinting at the Mafia, Chief Inspector. Or are you?"

"Perhaps I am. If it would make you see reason—"

"I've told you, it's no concern of mine. Unless Paul Granville is involved in some way, of course."

"You're trying to prove he murdered that girl."

"I'm trying to find the truth of the matter, whatever it is." He pushed back his plate. "Why should Whitehead want to harm me, after five minutes' conversation?"

"If he's been told of your . . . well, of your—"

"Meddling is my uncle's word, Chief Inspector. I make you a present of it."

"Meddling, then. *If* he's heard that, and *if* he thought you were taking too great an interest in his affairs—"

"That would mean he's connected in some way with the *Hazard Club*. That was the only thing we talked about."

"I've heard more unlikely stories."

"So have I. But this Eddie Baker of yours—"

"There is no known connection between him and the Club, if that's what you mean."

"No *known* connection. But either way—I already said this —it doesn't make sense."

"I daresay it will, when we have all the facts," said Sykes peaceably. "In the meantime, I'm telling you, watch your step, that's all."

"I'm grateful for your interest. Do you think I shall be allowed to deal with the brief from Miss Edison's solicitors in quite an orthodox way?"

"I can't tell you that, Mr. Maitland."

"Well, I shall just have to hope for the best. If my guardian angel's working overtime I should be quite safe now, don't you think? By the way, do you know anything about Oscar White-head?"

"If I did I wouldn't tell you," said Sykes emphatically.

"Now, I thought you trusted me."

"I don't want to encourage you, that's all."

"No. I see. I shouldn't mind betting—except that you seem to disapprove of it—that if you don't know anything about him you'll have a shot at finding out."

Sykes only smiled at that, and declined to be drawn any further. They talked of less controversial subjects while they drank their coffee, and parted at last, neither of them completely satisfied with the result of the interview.

III

Irene Brooke was small and slim and pretty in a rather anxious kind of way. She claimed to be an actress, but even after he had been talking to her for some time Maitland could not visualize her fitting into the hard, bright world of the stage. You needed to be tough to survive there . . . as tough as Meg was, for instance; though, come to think of it, she didn't look it either.

Irene admitted having given evidence at the inquest; they had wanted to know whether Cynthia was likely to have had the *Drowse* tablets in her possession, and she had told them No, it was most unlikely indeed. Quite impossible, really.

"Are you sure about that?"

"The way she felt about drugs . . . oh, yes, I'm quite sure. At least—" She broke off and looked at him in a worried way.

"Has something occurred to you, Miss Brooke?"

"No, only if Harriet had stayed the night and left them. She says she didn't—leave anything there, I mean, I know she stayed the night once or twice. And she's a very positive person, I'm sure she's right about that. And even if she had I don't think Cynthia would have kept them. She'd have given them back if she could, or else thrown them away."

"They must have asked you, too, in what sort of spirits Cynthia seemed when last you saw her."

"That was the Wednesday before—before she died. She was resting, you know, and she was just a little bit worried about her next part. Or not so much worried, really, as wanting a particular one and wondering if she had any chance at all of getting it."

"The leading role in *The Silent City*?"

"Yes, she read the book, and as soon as she heard it was being dramatized she said she'd like to be in it."

"And she knew Mr. Anketell, of course."

"Yes, he seemed . . . well . . . fond of her. Perhaps I shouldn't say that, I don't really know."

So Cynthia was discreet enough to keep her conquests to herself. "How did she feel when she knew he had given her the part?"

"Oh, but she didn't know. I mean, I don't know if he meant to or not, but if he did Cynthia had no idea of it."

"On the Friday afternoon. You didn't—"

This time she rushed in quite quickly. "I didn't see her after that, but she'd have phoned me. You don't know what that part meant to her, Mr. Maitland."

He reflected on the possibility that William Anketell had

been lying to him as he went to find Harriet Davis, who was modeling at Raymonde's that week. He had to wait until just after four o'clock, when the showing finished, and then for nearly half an hour while she removed her make-up, but she joined him at last and seemed to welcome the suggestion of tea.

There was a café two doors away, and Harriet chose a table by the window. She was a dark girl, a little sallow now that the heavy make-up was removed, and her main claim to beauty was the grace of her movements. He noticed with surprise that she had no inhibitions at all when it came to ordering muffins and cream cakes.

"I've just been talking to your friend, Miss Brooke," he said as the waitress left them.

"Irene . . . oh, dear!" She smiled a little, but the smile had no malice in it. "You'll have upset her again, I shouldn't wonder. She hated the inquest, you know."

"She tells me she's an actress."

"Quite a good one, too, once she forgets herself. But she suffers agonies from stage fright every single night."

"I can imagine, anyway, that the inquest was something of an ordeal for both of you."

"Not that so much, but because it was Cynthia. It was bad enough her dying, but . . . all that—"

"Do you think she was likely to have had *Drowse* in her possession, Miss Davis?"

"No, I don't. One time when she wasn't sleeping well I tried to get her to take some . . . they're quite harmless as long as you stick to the proper dose, and I told her that. But you'd have thought I was offering her straight poison the way she went on."

"So there is no question of her having yielded to a sudden impulse."

"I suppose not. It's a funny thing, I hadn't thought about that before."

"When she wanted to obtain them—"

"There's a chemist just across the street. I can't see why she should have gone any farther."

50

"A half-empty bottle. Don't you think she might have applied to one of her friends?"

"I should think they'd have asked questions. I should myself . . . knowing she had such strong feelings on the subject, you know."

"You didn't, youself, ever leave a bottle there by accident?"

"Irene asked me that. I suppose you got the idea from her. I didn't, and I couldn't have done so without knowing, I'm sure of that."

The waitress brought their tea, and they were silent until she went away. He asked her then, "When was the last time you saw Cynthia before she died?"

"It was on the Wednesday. Irene and I spent the evening with her."

"Just the three of you?"

"If you mean, was Paul Granville there, he wasn't."

"How did she seem that evening?"

"Much as usual. A bit nervy perhaps, because she'd just turned down a small part in one of Grossman's plays, but she said she couldn't tie herself up until she knew for certain about *The Silent City*."

"Was she hopeful about that?"

"On and off. I didn't say anything, but I was fairly sure she wouldn't get it."

"Why was that?"

"Because Willie Anketell had fallen for her."

"In that case—"

"He wanted her." She sounded impatient now. "I don't know if he'd have been very scrupulous about how he got her, most people aren't. But she was still emotionally involved with Paul."

He smiled at her. "That's one way of putting it. Tell me, then, was she happy in the relationship?"

"If you want to know what I think, she'd rather have been married. But of course it would have been treason to say so, in view of how Paul felt."

"In other respects—?"

"As far as I know she was completely satisfied."

"Did she tell you Mr. Anketell had given her the part she wanted?"

"I'm sure he hadn't."

"It was after you saw her. On the Friday afternoon."

"I don't believe it. She'd have let me know."

"Perhaps she wanted to tell Granville first."

"It can't have been that. I remember he said he'd seen her on the Saturday night, and she was alone all day Sunday as far as anyone knew."

"You mean, she'd have taken the opportunity of getting in touch with you."

"Of course." Between them, they had finished the muffins, and she reached out absent-mindedly for the largest of the cream cakes. "She didn't need the part, you know. I suppose Paul would have looked after her financially. But it meant a lot to her all the same, she'd have been quite delirious with joy if she'd got it."

"Not in a frame of mind to kill herself."

"Far from it. That's why I'm sure she didn't know."

"You don't agree with Lynn Edison, then?"

"Oh, no." She raised her eyes from her plate and gave him a smile. "I don't think I should dare admit it if I did."

"Between the two of us, with no witnesses."

"Even so. But I don't agree with Lynn, not at all."

"Not even so far as to think Cynthia might have been murdered?"

"Not even as far as that. I can't think of anybody but Paul who'd have had a motive."

"Some other flame of his," he suggested. "Or an admirer of hers, crazed with jealousy—"

"You make it sound like a game," she told him, reproving his light tone. "It would be too fantastic to think anybody wanted to murder her."

"If she'd quarreled with Granville, or if he'd told her he was

5 2

going to leave her . . . do you think after that she'd have bothered to tell you about the part?"

"How can I tell a thing like that?" But all the same she was giving the idea her attention. "She might have wanted company, to take her mind off things. Or she might have wanted to be left alone."

"Which do you think the most likely?"

She paused again, considering. "The first idea . . . yes, I think so. But you're talking as if she'd been given the part."

"According to Anketell he told her about it on Friday afternoon."

"That's the sort of thing it's easy to say now."

"Can you give me any reason why he should be making it up?"

"No, I can't."

And though he persisted a little longer with his questioning, she didn't seem to be able to tell him any more than that.

IV

Once she had finished a rather lengthy recital of how she had come all over queer when she found Cynthia Edison's body, Mrs. Somers, who had obliged the dead girl six days out of the seven, was really easier to talk to than either Irene or Harriet. She was so plainly pleased to see him, and to have the opportunity of airing her views. She had let herself into the flat at nine o'clock on the Monday morning, because Miss Edison wasn't one to get up early. "Which it was natural enough she'd like a lie-in, when you considered the heathenish hours she used to keep."

"You mean, when she was working?"

"Well, I wouldn't know, of course, about other times, but perhaps it got to be a habit. All I do know is, she was that sleepy in the morning—"

"But that Monday morning she wasn't in bed."

"No, there she was, sitting on the couch, only she'd fallen

back against the cushions, poor girl. I didn't take it in straight away, which was only to be expected, and I walked right up to her, and it was then I saw she was dead. I wasn't really in any doubt about it, but I rang the doctor, of course, and it was him who telephoned for the police. And one of the neighbors let me sit down in her room and gave me some tea, which I could do with after what I'd been through, as you might say."

"It must have been a great shock to you. Can you describe how the room looked when you got there?"

"Not when I got there. I was too taken up with that poor young thing. But afterward, after they'd taken her away, the police had me in there again, asking questions as if I'd something to hide, and they said they hadn't touched anything, and they made me look to see if anything had been moved."

"Tell me, then, what you saw."

"The curtains were drawn tight across the windows and the light was on. That should have told me straight off something was wrong, but somehow it didn't. And there was a magazine, open, on the couch beside where she'd been sitting. And there was the coffee pot, and sugar basin, and just one cup on the tray. She was very fond of coffee, well I told her often enough it wasn't good for her—"

"What was she wearing when you found her?"

"A neglidgy, she called it. She only bought it the day before, so it did seem a shame. She came in with it all excited, just as I was leaving on the Saturday morning, and I had to admit it was pretty, with the lace and all."

"Do you think her wearing it meant she was expecting somebody?"

"It might have, but she wasn't, was she? That's what I meant, it seemed pathetic like that she'd got all dressed up to die."

"Was there anything else about the sitting room?"

"Not really. The ashtray was full; they took it away with them, done up in a cloth like a pudding. And they made me look in the kitchen, but there wasn't a cup on the draining board, nothing like that."

"Hadn't she used any crockery during the weekend?"

"Oh, she'd have washed that up herself, she used to say she couldn't abide to see dirty dishes lying about. But I could tell she'd been upset, because one of the cups was hanging the wrong way around—"

"Mrs. Somers . . . excuse me . . . but is there a right way around to hang cups?"

"Only a habit she had, all of them facing left, as you might say. If I hung one the other way I've seen her straighten it . . . as if it mattered. But there, we can't all of us be sensible all the time."

"So you think she was upset when she washed up her dinner things?"

"No, her teacup, it must have been. Her after dinner coffee cup was still on the tray."

"Yes, of course. Did you tell this to the coroner?"

"I told the police, as was my duty. But I'm not one to put myself forward, and they never asked me again."

"I see. Thank you, Mrs. Somers." He rather thought, as he left her, that her evidence was the most interesting he had heard that day. And also, probably, the most useless, so far as convincing a jury went.

V

Johnny Lund was coming to supper, and had already arrived when Antony got home that night. As he went up the stairs he was regretting the impulse that had led to the invitation; he was tired, and his shoulder was aching, and one way and another he had had a surfeit of Lynn Edison's affairs for one day. But when he pushed open the door of the living room and found his wife and their guest sitting companionably in the firelight, with only the lamp on the writing table switched on, he began at once to feel better. One of Jenny's gifts was that she succeeded, without any apparent effort, in creating an atmosphere of tranquility (with very little help from either Antony or Sir Nicholas), and always he savored the moment of homecoming as one of the most precious things that he possessed. Sir Nicholas would have said that what really soothed him was the prospect of a drink, but that is perhaps unnecessarily cynical.

He went to stand in his favorite place with his back to the fire, and Jenny got up and poured sherry, and refilled Johnny's glass and her own. "I have been," he said, "asking questions all day. And answering a few as well."

"You ought to have let me come with you," Johnny told him.

"No." He sipped his drink, and placed it on the mantel behind him. "If we're to behave in an unorthodox fashion, we may as well go all the way. And people talk more freely without the distraction of a third person, don't you think?"

"I suppose they do. But Jenny's been telling me what happened last night—"

"With the best will in the world, Johnny, you couldn't have done anything to help. And in case you're still worried, Jenny love, if Chief Inspector Sykes is right our rock-throwing friend is already dead."

"You mean, there won't be any further attempts—?"

"I can't see why there should be." He told them, briefly, what Sykes had said . . . on that subject only.

"It was in the evening paper," said Jenny. " 'MAN SHOT DEAD ON BUILDING SITE' . . . something like that. Only of course I didn't know it was anything to do with you."

"Well, that's that! I can't make any sense of it myself."

"You went to the *Hazard Club*. Did you learn anything there?" Johnny asked.

"Oh, yes." He picked up his glass again, and went to sit in one of the wing chairs at the side of the hearth. "I learned, by observation, that Paul Granville smokes; fairly heavily, too."

"I don't see what good that will do. I don't see that it helps us at all," said Johnny with mounting indignation.

"I'm sorry." He was still addressing Lund, but his eyes were on Jenny's face. "There are two things outstanding. There's a chemist 'just across the street' from Guildford Place; find out if

Cynthia was a customer of theirs, and if she ever bought any *Drowse*."

"I've already been there. They knew her quite well, but she only bought cosmetics . . . things like that."

"Good. The other thing is to ask Lynn Edison whether Cynthia had told her she had got the part she wanted in *The Silent City*."

"But . . . had she?"

"So Anketell says."

"Well, I'm sure Lynn can't have known about it. She'd have been sure to tell us, because it's another argument against suicide, wouldn't you say?"

"I should. About that, Johnny . . . there are indications—"

"That it was murder?"

"That it might have been." He twisted in his chair, to take up the glass in his left hand. "It's all rather conjectural, I'm afraid."

"Are you going to tell me?" Johnny's impatience was barely kept in check.

"Of course. Anketell says he told her she was to have the part on the Friday before she died, and she was elated about it. You might read some confirmation of this in the fact that she bought herself a new negligee on Saturday morning . . . a sort of celebration that could have been. But both those girls you sent me to see were sure she couldn't have known; they said she would have been bound to tell them, couldn't possibly have kept it to herself. Anketell's evidence standing alone would be pretty impressive; I'm inclined to believe it myself. But we've no guarantee that Halloran won't get around to the subject in cross-examining Harriet and Irene, and unfortunately we need their evidence. That's one thing."

"Yes?"

"The others are even more nebulous. It's unlikely Cynthia would have got hold of a partly empty bottle if she'd set about obtaining *Drowse*. She left no letter, suicides usually do; the pad on the table could easily have been planted after she was dead. The fact that her fingerprints were on the bottle means nothing at all, that also could have been arranged. She was sitting on the sofa, not lying down; suicides usually make themselves as comfortable as they can. And then there's the tea-cup; it was put away the wrong way around."

"What on earth do you mean?"

"Just what I say. I'm quoting Mrs. Somers. Cynthia had a thing about the way she hung them up."

"I can just see the jury listening to that sort of stuff, can't you?"

"Stranger things have happened. It makes quite a vivid picture . . . the girl sitting alone, drinking coffee and reading *Woman's Review*; not expecting anyone—"

"How do you make that out?"

"Because she had to fetch another cup when the visitor arrived, and that's when the *Drowse* was stirred into her coffee. Of course, by the time Halloran's finished with it . . . no, I agree with you, Johnny, it's not nearly enough."

"I suppose it's the best we can do," said Johnny grudgingly.

"Unless we can get more from Granville in cross-examination."

"That means letting them state their case first."

"Yes, I think we must do that."

"But are we—? You said you wouldn't go into court with an accusation you didn't believe."

"Let's face it, there's nothing we can do unless Granville incriminates himself."

"Do you think he's likely to do that?"

"I don't, of course. But in fairness to Miss Edison I think we must try to show that the idea of murder isn't altogether out of the way. I shan't dare suggest to the jury directly that she was overwrought and her imagination ran away with her, but with any luck they'll get the idea . . . it could reduce the damages. Or if we're very lucky we might get Granville to admit there'd been a quarrel . . . something like that. That's really the best line to work on."

"What then?"

"In that case we forget all about murder, and hope the jury will conclude she was morally justified in what she said. I doubt if Halloran will let us get away with it, but if he does—"

"Contemptuous damages," said Johnny in a rapt tone. "And Lynn can't object—"

"I'm glad you think so."

"—because from her point of view it will be almost as good as a complete vindication of her ideas."

"Well, that'll be your job . . . to persuade her. If it comes to that, of course." He drained his glass and looked expectantly at Jenny. "That's all of shop for tonight, love. How soon can we eat?"

VI

Sir Nicholas was caustic when, later that evening, this plan of campaign was expounded to him. "But that wasn't what I wanted to talk to you about," he added. "Mallory tells me you were at Scotland Yard today."

"To be exact, I had lunch with Chief Inspector Sykes."

"What did he want?"

"To deliver a sort of gypsy's warning. But he gave me some information too."

"You were injured last night—"

"Not badly. Nothing to make a fuss about."

"—so perhaps the warning was justified." He was clearly extremely put out, and it took all Antony's ingenuity to divert him to a consideration of his own woes, specifically the probate case, the preparation of which did not seem to be coming along at all well.

THURSDAY, *29th February*

There was a fiction current among members of the bar that Mr. Justice Lovejoy was slow of understanding. The trouble was, he was a confirmed asker of questions, and rumor had it that he had even, on one occasion, queried the date of Christmas. He was a tall man, impressive in his robes, and old enough to be talking—and perhaps even thinking—of retirement. On the February day when he reached the case of Granville *versus* Edison in his list he was suffering from a head cold, and his temper was consequently somewhat impaired. He did not welcome the opportunity of seeing two television personalities at close quarters; they should have known better—defendant *and* plaintiff—than to air their differences in the courts. As for counsel, Halloran was a sound man, very sound; but Maitland was known to be unorthodox, and his lordship meant to keep a sharp eye open for any suggestion of the unseemly in his conduct.

Bruce Halloran, Q.C., was a close friend of Sir Nicholas Harding's, and as such well known to Maitland, even apart from their meetings in the courts. He was very dark, so that his wig looked almost startlingly white by contrast, and his figure was sufficiently portly to lend him a good deal of dignity. He greeted Maitland jovially as he came into court with his junior, and had unquestionably the air of a man who was very sure of the strength of his case. Maitland, who was leading his friend, Derek Stringer, looked pretty confident himself, but he would have been the first to admit—to any uninterested party—that this was a hollow sham. The weeks that had passed since Johnny Lund first brought Lynn Edison to see him had been peaceful enough, in that no further "accidents" had occurred, but neither had their case made any further progress. He felt himself hampered both by sympathy for his client and a certain nervous feeling that she might do anything at any time. Stringer, as was his custom, regarded the whole affair more philosophically, and was quite ready to take the rough with the smooth.

Neither the plaintiff nor the defendant showed any sign of uneasiness at all.

"The facts of the case are simple, and I shall not detain you long." That was Halloran, getting into his stride. Maitland stretched out his legs and closed his eyes, so that Johnny Lund, who had known him for ten years but never worked with him before, wondered uneasily if he was really asleep. Stringer—well accustomed both to his leader's attitude and to the reaction of the instructing solicitor—looked around and gave him an encouraging grin. Johnny smiled back, but found it impossible to relax. He tried, unsuccessfully, to catch Lynn Edison's eye.

"The defendant is young, and you may feel, ladies and gentlement of the jury, that this fact entitles her to your sympathy. Let me remind you that this libel was no matter of a few thoughtless words; it was a considered statement, made deliberately in the most damaging form possible, and as such can only be condemned." There'd be more in the same strain, thought Maitland, listening, and from Halloran's point of view it had the advantage of being true. He began to go over carefully in his mind again the line he himself intended to take. He rather

6 1

thought Halloran would have the laugh of him this time, and though he did not grudge him his victory he would deny it to him if he could.

" . . . but as to that, I shall let the facts speak for themselves," said Halloran inaccurately, having just finished a detailed recital of what he was about to prove. "It is estimated that two million people heard the libellous broadcast, but let me remind you that the case would be no different if one person only had heard it. There is this also to bear in mind: the plaintiff is a man in the public eye, well known, indeed famous, for his work in films and on television. As such, he is particularly vulnerable—"

("Good name in man or woman, good my lord," said Maitland *sotto voce,* and without opening his eyes.)

"—to an attack of this nature. Not only his personal reputation, but his very livelihood is at stake. I shall show you—" Thus Halloran, twisting the threads of his case together, to form an unbreakable whole. Maitland again appeared to have gone to sleep, and did not, in fact, rouse himself until the first witness was called.

The first witness was a young man with a shock of dark hair; he was wearing gray flannel slacks and a polo-neck sweater in a tasteful shade of buttercup yellow. Miss Edison's broadcast went out live, he said; as producer he would, of course, be listening and watching. Yes, of course he remembered the broadcast on the twenty-fourth of January. He thought he could quote from it verbatim. "Miss Edison said, 'And now I want to touch on a personal theme, the death of my sister, Cynthia. Those of you who have read of it will know that it has been dismissed as suicide, whereas in fact it was murder, and not by—'"

Maitland was on his feet. "May I make a correction, my lord? I am instructed that my client's actual words were 'deliberate and premeditated murder.'"

"If you wish the record to be changed, Mr. Maitland, we

shall certainly do so," said the judge, speaking rather thickly because of his cold.

"Thank you, my lord." Both Stringer and Johnny Lund were frowning, but if he could shake his opponent's confidence in any way . . .

"I'd forgotten, but of course that's what she said," the witness agreed. " 'Deliberate and premeditated murder,' she said, 'and not by some person unknown but by someone well known to all of you. Paul Granville.' And that was all I heard because I realized it was something that oughtn't to be going out, and I had the broadcast cut."

Halloran was thanking his witness. Maitland came to his feet again. "I do not wish to cross-examine, my lord. Perhaps it will save the court's time, and my learned friend's patience, if I inform you that we have no intention of denying the words that were said, or the fact that they were broadcast over the *Wessex* television network."

The judge sneezed. Halloran said, without any great show of pleasure, "In that case I shall, if your lordship pleases, dispense with any further evidence as to the libel and call Cyril John Roydon as my next witness."

Mr. Roydon's subject was listener surveys, and he quoted figures until Maitland's head spun. The outcome seemed to be that the figure of two million listeners which he had quoted was, if anything, on the conservative side. "Miss Edison's broadcasts were very popular indeed." Again the defendant's counsel did not cross-examine. An observer who did not know him well might have thought he was pleased with the way things were going.

He looked up with more interest, however, when Daniel Owen came into the witness box. Paul Granville's agent did not look any more impressive here than he had done when Roger Farrell pointed him out at the *Hazard Club*. A stocky man, who should have exuded self-confidence, he had instead an oddly ingratiating air. He had not heard the broadcast of January twenty-fourth himself, but the matter had soon been brought to his notice. Yes, he had gone with Paul Granville to see Lynn Edison. A mistake, he thought, but Mr. Granville had been anxious to do the right thing. Not that the gesture had been appreciated; she had repeated the charge of murder to his face.

"My lord! This is the first we have heard of slander."

"The matter seems immaterial, Mr. Maitland, as your client admits the libel."

"It is a question, my lord, whether evidence concerning this meeting between defendant and plaintiff should be heard."

"What do you say to that, Mr. Halloran?"

"It tends to show malice, my lord."

"Then I think, Mr. Maitland—"

"As your lordship pleases."

"Perhaps you will tell us, Mr. Owen—"

"Mr. Granville was upset . . . well, who wouldn't have been? He said he was sure there had been some mistake, and we'd go and see the girl to get it straightened out. But it was as I said, there was no question of an apology—"

"Even though Mr. Granville went out of his way to make things easy for her?"

"That's the way it was, so after that he had no alternative but to start proceedings, you see."

There was a little more detail given before Halloran had finished with his witness. Maitland came to his feet as his learned friend sat down.

"Why did you think this visit was a mistake?"

"It didn't seem it could do any good. She'd said what she meant very clearly. I thought it would only upset Mr. Granville all over again."

"He had been deeply disturbed by the statement?"

"It wasn't the kind of thing one likes to have said of one."

"No, indeed. But still he went to see Miss Edison."

"Yes."

"He hoped that she would retract what she had said?"

"He didn't want to be forced to take action—"

"All with the very best of intentions, of course."

"M'lud, if my learned friend is going to sneer—" said Halloran, surging to his feet.

"Nothing, my lord, was further from my thoughts," said Maitland, pained.

"I am glad to hear it," said the judge. And then, curiously, "What was in your mind, Mr. Maitland?"

"I thought perhaps Mr. Granville had wanted to find out what Miss Edison knew, my lord," Maitland told him, and waited in silence for the storm to blow itself out. The trouble was, Halloran knew him too well to be roused to any genuine wrath by his baiting.

"I have no further questions," he said, as soon as the tumult had died down.

The judge blew his nose like a trumpet call, and decided to adjourn.

I

The first witness the following morning was Leslie Baird, an unfortunate name, as it left some doubt in the mind as to the sex of its owner which his general appearance did little to allay. The uniform argued masculinity (a field marshal in the Ruritanian army, thought Maitland vaguely, an honor for which the wearer seemed rather young), but the shoulder length hair might have been taken as a contradiction.

Mr. Baird, for all his youth and his equivocal appearance, was as self-possessed as a witness could possibly be. He took the oath with the air of one humoring the children, and answered Halloran's questions without hesitation. His name . . . his address . . . his position as honorary secretary of the Paul Granville Fan Club.

"Did you hear the defendant's broadcast on January twenty-fourth?"

"Sure I did."

"And the reference to Mr. Paul Granville?"

"Why else would I be here?"

"What did you think when you heard that?"

"Like the chick was out of sight."

"I thought it was a *television* broadcast, Mr. Halloran," said Lovejoy querulously. His cold was a little better today, but still he didn't seem altogether happy.

"I—I think it means, m'lud—" said Halloran, looking wildly at his witness.

"She was up tight, but she knew what she was talking about," translated the witness amiably.

"Precisely," said Halloran, seizing with relief on the one part of this statement that he understood. "She was . . . you felt there must be something in her story?"

"Like it was for real."

"She said my client had murdered Cynthia Edison, and you believed her?"

"She couldn't tell a lie on television."

This was clearly intended as an affirmative reply, and Halloran sat down rather quickly, before the judge could again intervene. Maitland, on the other hand, got up with suspicious alacrity.

"Where were you, Mr. Baird, when you heard this broadcast talk?"

"In front of the eye."

"The *eye,* Mr. Halloran," said the judge in a plaintive tone.

"The eye . . . the box . . . the television," the witness told him kindly, without waiting for counsel's intervention.

"Were you at your own home?" Maitland asked.

"Sure we were."

"Can you remember how many people were present?"

"No, man, I was consumed by the eye."

"Even so,"—it sounded rather uncomfortable, he thought—"I should be grateful if you would try to remember."

"Five . . . six . . . ten—"

"And you all stopped talking to hear what Miss Edison had to say."

67

"Like we were tired. There'd been this happening—"

"What *is* a happening?" inquired Mr. Justice Lovejoy.

"An occurrence of some particular significance," Maitland told him. And added, after a short struggle with his better self, "It might be a fun thing, or a love-in, perhaps."

"What is a love-in?"

"I was hoping your lordship could tell me," said Maitland, crestfallen.

"Perhaps, m'lud, we should swear an interpreter," Halloran suggested.

"The witness appears to be speaking the English language," said the judge suspiciously, and addressed himself to Mr. Baird. "Do you understand what is going on?"

"Everything's cool, man—my lord," amended the witness hastily, losing his nerve for the first time.

"You really must keep your witness in better order, Mr. Halloran," said Lovejoy petulantly.

"If you would be kind enough to address the court in plain language, Mr. Baird—"

"I'll try," said the witness obligingly, "but it's not my bag."

"This happening, then," said Maitland. "You had been to a meeting, perhaps, or to a party?"

"What a trip! We were taking off a high—"

"Please, Mr. Baird!"

"Sobering up. Like we weren't drunk, man, just a bit turned up."

"You were too tired to talk, so you listened instead to the broadcast?"

"Have you ever seen Lynn?" This was clearly a rhetorical question; he paused to smile at the defendant. "I told you, she's out of sight."

"How long have you been secretary of the Fan Club?"

"Since the beginning of time."

"If you could make a more accurate estimate, Mr. Baird—"

"Three years . . . maybe."

"And you thought it was likely . . . this story that he had committed murder?"

"He was a friend, but Lynn was telling it."

"Was it *likely,* Mr. Baird?"

"Likely or not, it was Lynn on television, cheating on Paul."

"Cheating?" said Maitland hopefully.

"Squealing. Telling what she knew." And that, in a variety of ways, each more fantastic than the last, was all he could be induced to say.

The next witness to damage was slightly less colorful, as long as you kept your eyes from dwelling on his cravat. His name was Brian Stevenson: a man of about Granville's age, a close friend, he said. . . . Yes, he had heard the broadcast, he'd been quite horrified, but it never occurred to him that Miss Edison was speaking from anything but certain knowledge. Several people had spoken to him about the matter, they had all been equally shocked—

"I can appreciate my learned friend's desire to get something for nothing," said Maitland, coming to his feet in a hurry, "but surely the witness cannot speak to this of his own knowledge."

Halloran shrugged in a deprecating way, waved a hand toward the witness as if in invitation, seated himself with the air of one who has accomplished exactly what he set out to do, and left Maitland to get on with the cross-examination.

"Were you at your own home when you heard the broadcast?"

"Yes."

"Alone?"

"Yes, alone."

"Listening attentively?"

"Oh, yes, I have always found Lynn Edison's commentaries extremely interesting."

"Can you remember what else she spoke about that night?"

"No, not really."

"How long had she been speaking when she introduced this item about her sister?"

"About ten minutes, I should say."

"And you had listened from the beginning?"

"All the time."

"Yet you cannot remember one thing—"

"I expect the shock drove everything else out of my mind."

"The shock of hearing what she said about your friend?"

"That's right."

"A statement which you implicity believed?"

"I'm afraid I did."

"Do you believe it now?"

"Paul tells me—"

"Do you believe it now?"

"I don't know."

"How long have you known Paul Granville?"

"Ten years, just about."

"Been a friend of his all that time?"

"Certainly."

"Yet you had no more faith in him, when you heard this broadcast, than to become instantly convinced he was a murderer."

"She sounded very sure of herself."

"So you would rather trust Miss Edison's statement than your own knowledge of your friend."

"I didn't want to believe it."

"Do you know Lynn Edison?"

"Not well. I've met her, with Paul."

"I see."

"The thing is, her talks have always been very accurate."

"As far as your own knowledge goes, you mean."

"Yes, I suppose I do mean that."

"And this time nothing you knew of your friend seemed to make it unlikely that he was a murderer—"

"Oh, I didn't think it was *likely*—"

Maitland sat down and the witness's sentence trailed into silence. Halloran let him go.

Mr. Vincent Lucas was more impressive than either of his

predecessors, a man of fifty, a little inclined to stoutness, with a fine head of graying hair. Maitland looked at him with renewed interest as he took the stand; somewhere he had seen the witness before. And it wasn't at the Sloane Square branch of Bramley's Bank, of which he was just claiming to be manager, and at which Paul Granville had kept his account. . . .

"He was also a close personal friend, Mr. Lucas?" Halloran asked.

"I think I may say that. A close personal friend."

"On Wednesday, the twenty-fourth of January, you were listening to Lynn Edison's broadcast?"

"I was." He paused, but he needed no prompting to continue his statement. "Naturally, I had no inkling of what was to come. I was quite appalled when I heard what she said about her sister's death. I thought . . . I couldn't believe that she would make such a statement except from certain knowledge. I was very distressed indeed."

"I must ask you, Mr. Lucas, whether what you had heard affected your relationship with Paul Granville in any way?"

"How could it be otherwise? I had to think of the matter from a business point of view, as well as his friend."

That was the point at which Maitland started when he got his chance to cross-examine. "Are you concerned with the morals of your customers at the bank?"

"Only insofar as the account might be affected."

"If Paul Granville had asked for an overdraft—for instance —the day after you had heard the broadcast—?"

"I should have had to take it into consideration."

"But such a thing was unlikely to happen, wasn't it?"

"Very unlikely."

"So we are left with your friendship as the only thing that might be affected." As he spoke he remembered where he had seen the witness before . . . one of the group surrounding Granville the night he went with Roger to the *Hazard Club*. The chap he had thought looked like an ambassador . . . "How long have you known each other?"

"Since I went to the Sloane Square branch. About five or six years."

"Do you know Lynn Edison?"

"No."

"Yet you would prefer to take her word. . . . Were you alone when you heard the broadcast?"

"My wife was with me."

"But you were listening attentively, I take it."

"I always found her talks worth listening to."

"Accurate . . . well-informed?"

"Both those things."

"Were you acquainted with Cynthia Edison?"

"I had met her, several times, with Mr. Granville."

"Have you seen Mr. Granville since you heard the broadcast . . . since you thought he was a murderer?"

"Once only." (Confound the fellow, the answer came readily enough.)

"Where did this meeting take place?"

"At a club . . . the *Hazard Club*," he added, when counsel made no attempt to continue his questioning.

"A gaming house, owned by Mr. Granville?"

"So I believe."

"The bank has a financial interest, perhaps?"

"No indeed."

"Your visit was not on business then?"

"In a way. I was curious . . . I felt it to be my duty—"

"Even though there was a chance you would encounter Mr. Granville."

"Well . . . yes."

"And in fact, you say you did meet him."

"Yes."

"How did you feel?"

"Embarrassed."

"But still, you did not shun or avoid him?"

"I tried to behave as naturally as I could."

"You would describe yourself as a right-thinking member of society, I suppose."

"I hope so."

"But, although Miss Edison's statement had lowered Paul Granville in your estimation, you did not therefore try to avoid him."

"Except on that one occasion, I'm afraid I did."

"Are you quite sure of that, Mr. Lucas."

"Yes. Quite sure."

"I see. Thank you. That is all."

This time Halloran re-examined, but briefly. He seemed very sure of himself now.

II

Paul Granville was called after the luncheon recess. As Johnny Lund had foretold so gloomily, he was perfectly at ease in the witness box, and gave his evidence with an engaging air of frankness which annoyed Maitland very much indeed.

Yes, he had been the lessee of the flat in Guildford Place. Both he and Cynthia Edison had their careers to think of, and had felt it better to remain free of the marriage tie, but the understanding between them had been none the less enduring for that. He had seen her the day before she died, when she had been quite as usual; but he couldn't say he was surprised that a complete reversal of mood had taken place by the following day. She was an actress, and as so often happened with members of that profession such changes were of frequent occurrence. Certainly nothing in their relationship could have upset her, he thought she must have been worrying about her future . . . it meant a great deal to her, to succeed. He took sleeping tablets himself from time to time, but it was on his doctor's prescription. He had never used *Drowse*. And then—perhaps most damning of all—he had taken Lynn Edison out on several occasions before she introduced him to her sister. He wouldn't like to say that there might have been some jealousy involved, but he couldn't help wondering. . . .

That was as far as he got before Maitland's protest silenced him. Bruce Halloran sat down, well satisfied, leaving his opponent on his feet, to cross-examine.

"You last saw Cynthia Edison on the thirteenth of January . . . the day before she died?"

"I did."

"Did you quarrel?"

"No."

"Had you ever quarreled?"

"We didn't always agree."

"Was there any serious cause of dissension between you?"

"No. I don't think so."

"What, for instance?"

"I'm afraid I don't understand you."

"What did you disagree about?"

"Nothing serious. Small things, not worth remembering."

"Try to remember," counsel encouraged him. Granville made a show of hesitation.

"Sometimes she would have liked me to visit her more often than I actually could."

"Was she jealous?"

"Not exactly. I don't think you could call it that."

"Jealous of your work, perhaps."

"In a way, I suppose."

"And of the *Hazard Club*?"

"I don't—" (He didn't like the question; that was the first sign he had shown of a faint—a very faint perturbation.)

"You are the owner, aren't you?"

"Well . . . yes."

"And as such you went there most evenings, if you were not otherwise engaged."

"I like to keep an eye on things."

"Cynthia Edison did not accompany you?"

"No, she disliked gambling. Besides, after the theater—"

"But she was resting at the time of her death, wasn't she?"

"Yes. As I say, she didn't care for gambling."

"Is the Club open on Sundays?"

"It is."

"Would you say that, in general, if you were not visiting Cynthia Edison you would be likely to call in at the Club?"

"In general . . . I suppose . . . yes, I suppose you could say that, in general."

"But on the night she died you neither called on her nor visited the Club. You say you were at home . . . alone."

"That is quite correct. Of course, if I'd known she was depressed I'd have gone to her." (A good recovery, that; on the whole Paul Granville's round.)

"You were both alone that night. Was that perhaps because there had been one of those disagreements between you?"

"No, nothing like that."

"What was the reason then?"

"No particular reason."

"When did your doctor prescribe a drug to make you sleep?"

"I'm afraid I don't remember."

"Before, or after, Cynthia's death?"

"Well . . . after."

"And before that—"

"I didn't take anything," said Granville quickly.

"Tell me about the last time you saw Cynthia Edison."

"I don't . . . what is there to tell?"

"How did she seem?"

"In good spirits."

"No worries of any kind?"

"None that she spoke of."

"She had turned down the offer of a part, hadn't she, in the hope of a better one in *The Silent City*?"

"That is correct."

"Didn't that worry her?"

"She was . . . a little concerned about it."

"Did she mention the matter, that last night?"

"I don't remember. I think perhaps she did."

"She didn't tell you that the part she wanted had been offered to her the day before?"

"No. She certainly would have told me—"

"It seems odd that she did not do so. I shall be bringing evidence to show that she had been offered and accepted the part."

"I don't . . . I can't believe it." (That worried him, too.)

"If you had quarreled, of course, that might explain things."

"We did not quarrel."

"Being offered the part would have made a difference to her state of mind, you think?"

"Of course it would."

"So if you didn't quarrel—"

"I have already told you that we did not."

"—you would think it reduced the probability of suicide?"

"If it was true. But I think you must accept—" He broke off, and gave counsel a doubtful look.

"What must I accept?"

"That she was a creature of moods. Changeable."

"But surely not without cause. If she was happy in her relationship with you—"

"That, at least, I am sure of."

"It must give you great satisfaction," said Maitland ironically, and wondered if Halloran would object again to his "sneering." "If, as I say, she was happy in her relationship with you, and happy about her career, it is a little difficult to understand why she should kill herself . . . don't you think?"

"She would have told me about the part."

"The fact remains that she did not."

"No."

"Let us go back to the last time you saw her, the night before she died." On the whole it seemed that that was the point on which Granville was most vulnerable. If something he had said, or done, had thrown Cynthia into despair . . . but it wasn't going to be as easy as that, of course. Maitland was still pursuing the matter, with an increasing feeling of unreality, when Mr.

Justice Lovejoy had an unfortunate fit of coughing, and adjourned in a hoarse voice, and rather earlier than was usual.

<h1 style="text-align:center">III</h1>

"Halloran tells me he's going to win his case," said Sir Nicholas Harding, who was dining with the Maitlands that evening. He had just embarked on his second glass of sherry, and sounded benevolent and at peace with the world.

"Halloran," said Antony, "is probably right."

"Probably?"

"No . . . of course. Certainly right."

"I told you you shouldn't touch it."

"I've lost cases before today. I don't even know whether I ought to win this one, and in the circumstances I've got to give some consideration to that."

"I thought you had made up your mind—"

"The girl may have committed suicide because of a quarrel with Granville, but I think she was more probably murdered. If she was, I imagine he was the murderer, but that's just on the principle of suspecting the husband, you know."

"Were they married?"

"No, but it seems to have been . . . well . . . a settled relationship."

"Of six months' duration."

"Nine, as a matter of fact. Anyway, there isn't a smell of motive of any kind."

"Even an actor, I suppose, would be unlikely to commit murder without reason."

"I just mean, if there is one I don't know it. For that matter, even an actress wouldn't kill herself, without cause."

"What will happen to Lynn?" said Jenny, who had just come back from the kitchen.

"I don't know. I don't think," he added carefully, "that the outlook is really so rosy, do you?"

"Unless she marries Johnny."

"No, really, love, on the strength of one date for dinner!"

"He's seen more of her than that."

"Oh, has he? Then perhaps he'll be ready to pick up the pieces, if she isn't too damned independent to let him."

"I told you," said Sir Nicholas again, maddeningly superior, but he was answering the tone rather than the words. "I told you at the start that you shouldn't touch it."

That was on Friday evening, before the phone call came at about a quarter to ten. It was Lynn Edison's voice that greeted Antony when he lifted the receiver and announced his presence. "I'm sorry to bother you, Mr. Maitland, but I couldn't get hold of Johnny." She sounded breathless, quite unlike her usual self.

"That's all right."

"Could you possibly come to the Lennox Street police station?"

"Now?"

"Oh, yes, now . . . please!"

"If you need me. Why?"

"Paul Granville has been shot. They haven't exactly arrested me," said Lynn, picking her words, "but I should think they're going to, any minute now."

IV

He went, of course. And Sir Nicholas refrained from saying "I told you so" again, when he saw his nephew's expression. He found Lynn, looking mutinous, in one of the waiting rooms, a very bleak and cheerless place. "I was right, wasn't I?" she demanded as he went in. "I didn't *have* to say anything until you got here, did I?"

He felt a slight sinking of his spirits, which—if the truth were told—were already depressed. "You were within your rights, certainly. But now you'd better tell me what's been happening."

"I did tell you. Paul Granville has been shot."

"Is he dead?"

"Oh, yes." She shuddered. "It was rather horrible, really. He was shot through the head."

7 8

"Did you do it?"

"Of course not!"

"But you were there?"

"Yes, I—I found him."

"What on earth—? Was it suicide?"

"The police don't seem to think so. I suppose it couldn't have been really . . . the gun wasn't in his hand, or anywhere near him." She hesitated a moment. "Mr. Maitland, where is Johnny?"

He sat down then, on the corner of the table. "I'm sorry if I'm a poor substitute, but you'd better tell me. Exactly what happened, from the beginning." But before she could answer him the door opened and two men came into the room.

The Divisional Detective Inspector was in the lead, a man he had never seen before. And bringing up the rear (but not, if Maitland knew it, prepared to be in any way backward in the questioning that was to follow), Detective Chief Inspector Conway of the Criminal Investigation Department, New Scotland Yard, whom he knew very well indeed. Chief Inspector Conway had a thin face, a pugnacious jaw, and a tongue that was probably no less sarcastic now, in spite of his recent promotion. His disposition had never been sunny, and his present tight-lipped look was natural to him, but perhaps accentuated a little by the realization that his path and Maitland's were again to cross.

"Perhaps *now* you will be ready, Miss Edison, to answer our questions," he said, coming up beside the D.D.I.

"We are quite ready," said Antony, and spared a thought for the confusion he was inviting if Lynn hadn't told him the truth. He was still sitting on the table, and now he began to swing his foot. "It isn't really polite," he added, "to look at me as if you'd come across a slug in your salad."

"I didn't expect to see you here, Mr. Maitland."

"No, how should you? Unfortunately, Miss Edison's solicitor isn't available at the moment, so if I can help her—and you, of course—I am quite at her service."

Conway gave him a hard, suspicious look. "Thank you. I

have had experience before now of your idea of being helpful," he said.

The local inspector looked from one of them to the other. He was a heavy man, several inches taller than his colleague. "We'd be more comfortable in my office," he said, and seemed surprised at the readiness with which they followed him.

His statement had been perhaps an exaggeration. It was a shabby room, and it reeked of cigarette smoke, and the chairs were hard and uncompromisingly utilitarian. Lynn sat facing the desk, and Antony pulled up a chair beside her. "Now, Miss Edison, before we begin I must warn you—" They were in earnest then. Not a matter that could be shrugged off with some facile explanation. The question was . . . did she, or didn't she? At that moment he would have given a good deal to know.

Having issued his warning, the divisional inspector sat back and waited for the man from Scotland Yard to take over. Conway said, "What were you doing at Paul Granville's flat this evening, Miss Edison?" His tone was noncommittal now, but his eyes were sharp and watchful. The explanation had better be a good one.

"I went there to see Paul." She had herself well in hand, but Maitland thought he could detect the faintest suggestion of a tremor in her voice.

"So I had supposed. In the circumstances, wasn't that rather odd?"

"In what circumstances, Chief Inspector?" asked Maitland, before the girl could answer.

"Considering that your client was being sued by Paul Granville for libel. That could hardly have formed a very friendly background for their discussion."

"Hadn't you better wait for what Miss Edison has to tell us, before making up your mind?"

"Do you mean to allow her to answer?"

"Yes, certainly. In the circumstances, Miss Edison—" Of course, Conway was bound to have the libel action in mind; he only hoped he had given Lynn time to consider her reply.

However that might be, she answered readily enough. "Paul asked me to go."

"A social visit?"

She flushed a little at the sardonic tone. In the harsh light a worried frown showed between her eyes. "No, of course not. He said . . . the man who rang—"

"Not Mr. Granville himself then?"

"No. I thought perhaps it was Danny Owen; I've met him, and of course I heard him in court, but I don't think I'd recognize his voice. Or it might have been Paul's valet. He said, 'Mr. Granville would appreciate it if you would call on him this evening,' and of course I asked him why."

"Did he tell you?"

"Yes, in a way. He said, 'He has a communication to make to you. Something it would be in your own interest to hear.' I was curious, of course, so I went."

"Without any further questions?" Lynn shook her head. "Let me remind you, Miss Edison, this was a man you had accused of murder."

"I didn't think he'd want to murder me. Certainly not in his own flat."

"At what time did you receive this message?"

"At about half-past eight."

"What then?"

"I told you. I went to Leinster Court."

"In a little more detail, please."

"Well . . . I got my coat and my handbag, and I went by tube, it took me about twenty minutes, I should say."

"And then?"

"I went up to the fourth floor. Paul's flat is at the end of the corridor, and the door was slightly open."

"Wasn't that rather odd?"

"The whole situation was odd," said Maitland, on whom the reiterated question was having an irritating effect. "Let us admit that right away. But you are questioning Miss Edison as to facts, Chief Inspector, not as to her opinions."

Conway compressed his lips into an even tighter line. "Very well," he conceded. "The door was slightly open. Did you go in?"

"Not immediately. I rang the bell, and then I knocked. But nothing happened, and I thought perhaps the door had been left open on purpose, because he was playing records, for instance, and it might be difficult to hear. So I went in."

"And found?"

"The hall is long, and rather narrow. The sitting room door is on the left . . . sitting room . . . study . . . I don't know what he called it. It's a bit of both really. I called out, first, and then . . . he was sitting in a wing chair with his back to the door, and I could just see his arm. And there was a record playing, I didn't recognize what it was. So I went into the room, and found him. And the music stopped. It was the end of the record, of course, but it seemed . . . eerie, somehow—" The sentence trailed into silence, but after a moment she added, with finality, "That's all!"

"On the contrary, Miss Edison, it is hardly the beginning. You went into the room, until you could look down on him—"

"It was horrible! I saw at once that he was dead. His face—"

"What did you do?"

"I think I just stood staring for a moment. I know I wondered whether I was going to be sick. And then I knew I must call the police, so I looked around for the telephone. That's when I saw the gun, near the fender. But before I could do anything, Danny Owen came in, so he did the telephoning, after all."

"Where did Mr. Owen come from?"

"From outside. That's what he said, anyway, and he had his overcoat on, so I suppose it was true. And he said he'd found the door open, just as I had done. But he thought . . . he seemed to think . . . he looked at me as if I had killed Paul. I hadn't thought until I saw him looking at me. . . . I suppose it was silly, but I hadn't thought till then that anybody could suspect me."

For a moment Antony thought Conway was going to permit himself a smile at this ingenuous statement. "You'd better tell me, Miss Edison, exactly what passed between you."

"Well, he couldn't see Paul from where he was standing . . . only his arm. And he asked me, 'What are you doing here?' and then he said, 'Paul?' as if he was puzzled, and came across the room quickly until he could see for himself. And then for a moment he just looked at me. . . . I told you about that. And I said, 'I only just got here.' And he went across to the telephone, but he kept his eyes on me the whole time, as if he thought I might try to run away. That's all, really. We just waited in silence until the first policeman arrived."

"You were still wearing your gloves when Mr. Owen first saw you."

"Yes, it was a cold night, and I hadn't had time to take them off."

"Did you recognize the gun?"

"Of course I didn't. I've never even seen one, except in museums."

"Then I suppose you will tell me you have never learned to fire one."

"I shall have to tell you that if you ask me, because it's true."

"I see. How do you think the libel case is going?"

"Facts, Chief Inspector," Maitland reminded him. "The question, however, is in any case an academic one . . . now."

"That was exactly my point, Mr. Maitland. If the case was going badly for the defendant—"

"Nothing of the kind."

"—murdering the plaintiff would have been one way of retrieving the situation, would it not?"

"A rather drastic one," said Maitland dryly. "In any case, I do not admit—"

"I didn't expect you to," said Conway, almost as though he was relieved to find his worst fears well founded. "All the same—"

"Have you considered how complicated it would be to suggest such a motive in court?"

"That need not concern us. Now, Miss Edison, we come to another point. How long had you known Paul Granville?"

"About a year."

"Is it true that during the first three months, say, of that period he was extremely attentive to you?"

"I don't . . . quite . . . know what you mean."

"It is really very simple. Did he act as your escort on a number of occasions . . . take you out to dinner, to the theater . . . buy you flowers?"

"I suppose you've been talking to Danny Owen. Certainly he took me about quite a lot."

"You were on good terms with him then, at that time."

"He was a pleasant companion. There was never any suggestion of anything more."

"What happened to break up this pleasant association?"

"Nothing special. It just died a natural death, I suppose."

"Unlike Paul Granville." Lynn pressed her lips together, as though to stop some indiscretion, and gave her head a shake. "I think you are not being quite frank with us, Miss Edison. Did not Mr. Granville's attentions cease after you had introduced him to your sister?"

"We don't care for that question, Chief Inspector," said Maitland, as the girl hesitated over her reply.

"Very well. We will go back, instead, to your actions this evening, Miss Edison. You were at your own home when the phone rang, at about—"

"Eight thirty."

"Thank you. Please tell me again, exactly what was said. . . ."

V

It was past one o'clock when Antony got back to Kempenfeldt Square. He found Jenny reading the newspaper in bed, but she put it down when he went in. The headlines shrieked up at him as he crossed to the foot of the bed. . . . POUND IN DANGER. . . . £300,000 TAKEN FROM CITY BANK. . . . TWO FOR TRIAL ON SECRETS CHARGE. Tomorrow there would be a new sensation.

"What happened, Antony?" asked Jenny anxiously.

"Granville is dead. They've arrested Lynn."

"Oh, no!"

"Oh, yes, I'm afraid. I ought to telephone Johnny."

"He rang up about an hour ago. Lynn must have left some sort of a message that alarmed him. I just said something had come up, and you were dealing with it. I didn't think it would do any good for him to start worrying tonight."

"I'll call him at breakfast time." He pulled off his tie, and threw it vaguely in the direction of the chair by the fireplace. "I think I need a drink, love. Can I get you anything?"

"No, thank you." She waited patiently while he went into the living room to forage, but was ready with her questions as soon as he came back to the bedroom again. "When was Paul Granville shot? I mean, hasn't it all happened rather quickly?"

"The trouble is, Lynn was there. She says she found him, and then Danny Owen walked in while she was still wondering what to do."

" 'She says' . . . don't you believe her?"

"I don't know. She has a tale about getting a telephone message from Granville asking her to go and see him. It sounds as phony as hell."

"What on earth will Johnny do?"

"It's Lynn you should be worrying about at the moment. I can't make up my mind whether to believe her, or not."

"As a client—"

"Oh, as a client it's simple. Everything she says is gospel truth, of course. What I can't decide, you see, love, is whether this is one of the times I ought to meddle in the preparation of the case; or whether I should stick to my brief and just do the best I can with it in court."

"If you aren't sure—" She broke off there, and sat looking at him for a moment, and then said apologetically, "I'm sorry. Not being sure works both ways, doesn't it?"

"That's just it. I'll see her again tomorrow . . . with Johnny, but without Inspector Conway; perhaps the answer will seem more obvious then."

"*Not* Inspector Conway?"

"I'm afraid so. He's no fool, you know, and he's already got it worked out that the libel action died with Granville, and therefore Lynn had a motive as big as a house."

"Meg likes her," said Jenny inconsequently. Antony got up purposefully, and began to shrug himself out of his jacket.

"I can't think of anybody whose opinion I'd rather distrust," he said.

SATURDAY, *2nd March*

I

John Lund, apprised of the situation by telephone the following morning, was inclined to incoherence, but by the time he arrived in Kempenfeldt Square he had his feelings more or less in command. By eleven o'clock they were closeted with Lynn Edison, who looked as though she had spent a sleepless night. "We want to hear everything that happened yesterday evening," Lund said.

"Hasn't Mr. Maitland told you?" she asked in a resentful tone. "He must have heard it half a dozen times."

"*Ad nauseam*," Antony agreed cheerfully. "Still, we might come across something that was left unsaid, you know."

"I don't see . . . oh, very well!" she said when Johnny seemed about to intervene again. And then, "I'm sorry to be so ungracious. It's just that I find I don't like the idea very much, that I can't get out."

"We want to help you," said Johnny, with a helpless look at his companion.

"That goes without saying," Maitland agreed. "To begin with, I wouldn't say the police thought very much of your story, would you?"

"I don't think they believed a word of it."

"Exactly. They were questioning you from that point of view; we, on the other hand, start by assuming your innocence."

"I wasn't sure—"

"What, Miss Edison?"

"That you believed me either."

He was still in two minds about that. "Try to convince me, then," he said, smiling at her. "What were you doing last night when the phone call came?"

"I was reading."

"That means you were alone."

"Yes, of course."

"Tell me about the voice then. Could it have been Granville himself?"

"Why ever should Paul pretend to be somebody else?"

"To stop you asking questions, perhaps."

"Well . . . I don't think—"

"You sound doubtful."

"No, not really. It's just that I'd never considered it before." She thought about it for a moment. "It was a queer voice . . . flat . . . not much character in it."

"Was the man concerned speaking naturally, or had he assumed an accent for the occasion?"

"Why should he do that?"

"As a disguise, in case you could identify him later. If it was the person who shot Granville—"

"Oh, no! I don't think that for a moment." She looked from one of them to the other. "I only wondered . . . what do you think Paul wanted?"

"I can't imagine. What do you usually say when you answer the phone?"

"Usually just 'hallo.' "

"Is that what you said last night?"

"I expect so." She was beginning to sound impatient.

"And how did the caller respond?"

"I don't think I remember."

"Did he say, 'Miss Edison?' or did he just plunge straight into the message?"

She wrinkled her forehead over that. "I think he said, 'Is this Miss Edison speaking?' And I said 'Yes,' and *then* he said about Paul wanting to see me."

" 'Mr. Granville would appreciate it if you would call on him this evening.' "

"You have a good memory, Mr. Maitland."

"And you said, 'Why should I?' or something like that—"

"And he said, 'He wants to talk with you. It would be in your own interest to hear what he has to say.' "

"And so you went."

"I told you . . . I was curious."

"Naturally. But you must have formed some opinion. What did *you* think Paul Granville had to tell you?"

"I thought perhaps . . . I was afraid I'd been wrong. I thought perhaps he knew something about Cynthia that I hadn't known."

"Something that had made her want to kill herself?"

"Yes." She wasn't looking at him now. Her eyes were fixed on a point on the wall somewhere above his left shoulder. "Do you think I haven't wondered sometimes if I hadn't made a dreadful mistake? And yesterday, when he was giving evidence, he sounded so self-assured."

"You felt there might be something to be said, after all, for his point of view?"

"It made me want to hit him," said Lynn frankly. "But it made me wonder, too."

"So you went . . . of course," he added, forestalling her. "We needn't dwell on the journey, nobody disputes you made it. Was your handbag large enough to have held the gun you saw?"

"I should think so." She was looking at him now, and then her eyes turned for a moment to Johnny Lund. "I didn't—"

"No, we're assuming that . . . remember? You'll have to find out about the weapon, Johnny." He turned back to Lynn again. "It may have belonged to Granville. If not, they'll try to prove you might have had access to it. A war souvenir . . . your father was in the forces, perhaps."

"In the Army. The Durham Light Infantry."

"Your parents are both dead, aren't they?"

"Yes."

"Is there anyone—a close relative, or friend—who might know what your father brought home in the way of souvenirs?"

"I can't think of anyone. I'm sorry."

"Never mind. It would be negative evidence at best. We can't prove you didn't own it, but they can't prove you did. Now, do you think anybody heard you, banging on the door?"

"I should think they could have done, there's another flat quite near. But nobody came out to see."

"Something else to find out about." He saw Johnny was making a note, and went straight on to his next question. "Had you ever been to Granville's flat before?"

"Yes, twice."

"Tell me—"

"Once was to a party. And once was on a Sunday when we were going into the country, but it rained and rained, so we stayed at home instead."

"I see. Did the man who spoke to you seem to know that?"

"I don't know. He did give me directions, and told me to take the tube to Queensway, but that doesn't mean anything really."

"Think of the flat, then . . . as you saw it before, as you saw it last night. Was anything different?"

"Not that I noticed."

"The door was open, you say?"

"Yes. About six inches."

"And the door to the living room?"

"That was wide open."

"You could hear the music from the corridor, then?"

"Yes. I think that's really why I went in."

"And Granville was sitting in a high-backed chair with his back to the door?"

"I could just see his left arm, hanging down rather limply. Only it didn't strike me then that there was anything wrong."

"Had he been sitting down when he was shot?"

"How on earth could I know that?"

"If he'd been standing the force of the shot might have knocked him back into the chair, but he'd have fallen all of a heap, not . . . well, not neatly."

"I suppose he was sitting down then. He looked quite natural . . . except for his head." She stopped, biting her lip, but her eyes were curious. "Does that tell you anything?"

"Not really. Someone he knew, or whom he had a good reason for admitting . . . we could assume that anyway. Now, think about the room. Was everything just as usual?"

"As far as I know. The bureau was open, and the telephone had been moved to stand on the—on the writing surface, instead of on the top. That's why I didn't see it straight away."

"Nothing else?"

"Not that I can think of."

"Danny Owen. When you heard him speak, did you still think the phone call might have been from him?"

"It could have been, I think. I haven't a very good ear for voices. But when I asked him he said he hadn't seen Paul before that day."

"If it was a ruse to get you there—"

"I don't know why you should think that. It was just a coincidence, that's all."

"You said, if you remember, that you didn't talk to Owen at all."

"Well, I'd forgotten. And that was all that was said."

"Did he behave naturally? Was he surprised?"

"He seemed to be, but mainly he was suspicious."

"Was he wearing gloves?"

"He was carrying them in his hand, and he dropped them on the open flap of the bureau when he picked up the phone."

"You were still wearing yours?"

"Yes. I don't think it's so instinctive a thing in a woman as in a man, to take them off."

"And there was nothing else you noticed?"

"Nothing . . . nothing! I don't like thinking about it at all, don't you see?"

"I'm sorry. I'm afraid you're not going to be allowed to forget it, just yet."

"No, I suppose . . . I know you're trying to help."

"As a matter of fact, I am." He got up as he spoke, and stood looking down at her. She thought his look was skeptical until he spoke, and then she wasn't sure. "One way or another," he said, "we've got to get you out of this."

II

He said as much to his uncle when they met at luncheon, and Sir Nicholas looked at him curiously. "That sounds as if you've made up your mind. Is it intuition, or bias, or what?" He answered himself before Antony could reply. "One thing I'm sure of, it isn't reason."

"As a matter of fact, I have a very good reason for thinking her innocent."

"For instance—"

"Well—"

"It's Inspector Conway's case, isn't it? Are you sure you haven't decided to meddle just to annoy him?"

"You ought to know me better than that, Uncle Nick," said Antony incautiously; which was asking for trouble, but fortunately Sir Nicholas's interest had been short-lived.

"We're in court on Monday," he said. "You know my client—"

"The 'singularly ill-favored' one?"

"That's right. I suppose you'll have to put in an appearance before Lovejoy, as a matter of form."

"I shall. Derek and Johnny can look after Lynn in the magistrate's court."

"Well, when you've finished, take a look in at our little affair. The jury may well believe my client did not influence the testator by her beauty, but I cannot guarantee they will not think she terrorized him into compliance."

Jenny said nothing at all. She had been, throughout the meal, unusually silent, even for her. A fact of which her husband was only too well aware.

III

Saturday afternoon was perhaps not the most propitious time to seek an interview with Chief Inspector Sykes. Antony delayed until half-past three, and then yielded to temptation and telephoned the detective's home. "Come and have tea with us, you and Mrs. Maitland," said Sykes, not at all put out by what another man might have regarded as persecution. Maitland thanked him, and rang off.

There were advantages in the arrangement; for one thing, it meant that they could take the car. Antony had not driven himself since the injury to his shoulder that had made the exercise so uncomfortable as to be almost impossible. Sometimes he cursed the disability, but mostly he took it philosophically enough, except when his shoulder was particularly painful, or when any well-meaning acquaintance ventured to commiserate with him.

He was not without curiosity to see where Sykes lived, but once they arrived he could visualize him in no other setting. Between the Chief Inspector and his wife there was that odd, elusive resemblance that sometimes exists between two people who have been happily married for many years. Their home, with its neatly dug garden (and not a leaf in sight, there must be a compost heap somewhere) seemed an entirely appropriate background. It was a comfortable, placid place, that gave the impression, not that it did not know the everyday shocks of living, but that it was in some way impervious to them. Jenny was ushered into the sitting room, but soon found herself following Mrs. Sykes into the kitchen, where she was allowed to keep an eye on the crumpets that were toasting under the grill; Antony and the Chief Inspector went into the dining room to talk.

The electric fire had been switched on in anticipation, and the room was already warm. "Well now, Mr. Maitland," said Sykes, seeing his visitor comfortably settled and seating himself in his turn, "what seems to be the trouble?"

"Have you heard what happened to Paul Granville?"

"There was a *Stop Press* in the paper this morning. I haven't been in to the office today."

"Did the *Stop Press* also tell you that Lynn Edison has been charged with the murder?"

"Your client in the libel case? Now, I do find that interesting, Mr. Maitland. I do, indeed."

"It's Conway's case, he's jumping to conclusions as usual. No, that's not fair," he added quickly, as Sykes seemed about to interrupt him. "He had a very good reason for arresting her. She was caught in what must have seemed almost *flagrante delicto*. It just so happens she didn't do it, that's all."

"Hmmph."

"That's what my uncle said."

"What, Mr. Maitland?"

"Was I sure I hadn't made up my mind about it, just to annoy Conway? I can see the fairness of that, it's just what I might have done. But as it happens I know she's innocent."

"That's putting it rather strongly, isn't it?"

"I don't think so. If it's an act of faith, I've a reason for it."

"Are you going to tell me—?"

"I don't think so. Not at this stage, Chief Inspector." (The truth was, to anyone else, the inference he had drawn would seem to be on impossibly flimsy grounds.) "But as things are, she'll be found guilty. I won't let that happen if I can help it."

"You'll forgive me for wondering . . . where do I come in?"

"Someone else killed him, therefore someone else had a motive. I'm still interested in the *Hazard Club*."

"I see."

"You were going to make some inquiries about Oscar White-head," said Antony encouragingly.

"That won't help you, Mr. Maitland. The results were purely negative."

"You mean, he hadn't got a record in the States?"

"No." He paused a moment, to consider the propriety of what he was about to say. "I don't think there's any harm in telling you: he's a lawyer, though he's more or less given up his practice for the last two or three years."

"But he told me his business was gambling. I thought he must come from Las Vegas . . . somewhere like that."

"No, New Jersey. When I said he had more or less retired I should have added that he was occupying himself exclusively with one client's affairs."

"Who—?"

"A man called Santinelli."

"A gangster!" said Maitland, suddenly alert.

Sykes looked amused, but shook his head at him. "A man of many interests, according to my information, none of which has ever been proved to be illegal."

"Oh . . . well! The practice of the law brings you in touch with all sorts of people," he added reflectively.

"So it does."

"What's he doing here, anyway? No . . . don't tell me . . . I realize you don't know. I shall just have to find out for myself, that's all."

"Mr. Maitland—"

"I know, you've warned me once. But if Whitehead is as blameless a character as you would have me think, there's nothing to worry about . . . is there?"

"I wouldn't say that . . . not exactly. Things have a nasty habit of happening when you're about. You'll agree to that."

"I suppose so. All the same—"

"You've some reason for suspecting Whitehead?"

"I think he's concerned, at least, in what's been going on. I can't go any farther than that."

"What are you going to do?"

"I haven't the slightest idea. Persuade Uncle Nick to take the case, for one thing." (This was the least of his troubles, and he knew it.) "Then approach it, I suppose, from the other end . . . Paul Granville and his friends and acquaintances."

"That sounds as good an approach as any," said Sykes cautiously.

"I'm being sensible, you ought to approve. But before we go any farther, Chief Inspector . . . what about Eddie Baker?"

"What about him?"

"The man who was murdered on the demolition site. Who may or may not have heaved half a brick at me. You remember."

" 'appen I do." That was Sykes, metaphorically retreating into the attic and pulling the ladder up after him.

"You probably know a bit more about him now than you did then."

"Yes, I think that's true enough."

"Can you tell me—?"

"What do you want to know?"

"Anything . . . everything. Did you ever connect him with the *Hazard Club*?"

Sykes smiled. "Nothing like that, Mr. Maitland. Nothing like that at all."

"Then what?"

"We got our first proof that he'd been mixed up in a crime, when it was too late to do us any good, as you might say."

"What did you find?"

"A fingerprint that tallied with one of his."

"Well, where—?"

"You'll have read about the series of bank robberies that have been in the news in the past six months."

"Of course I have. Are they a series, though?"

"There are certain characteristics that they have in common. Mainly, an extreme ruthlessness and disregard for human life.

96

On each occasion they have shot, and generally killed, one of the bank staff, or some innocent bystander."

"*Pour encourager les autres.* I see."

"There is also the method. A car stolen for the job, and later abandoned. Four masked men, each of them armed. The orders to the cashiers . . . hands on head, and stand well back from the counter. It's the getaway car that concerns us, though. About four months ago they slipped up for the first time, and a print was left inside the glove compartment that didn't belong to the owner or any of his family or friends. As though the driver had got nervous waiting, and looked in there for a cigarette. Something like that."

"You're telling me the driver was Eddie Baker?"

"That's only surmise. It seems he was concerned in some way with the crime."

"But then, why should he . . . what possible motive could he have for trying to knock me out?"

"I don't know that, Mr. Maitland, and it seems I must accept that you don't know either. I've been wondering whether one of your recent clients might have been in some way implicated."

"If they were I know nothing of it, and I can't see that it would constitute a motive—"

"I suppose not. But that's all I can tell you about Eddie Baker."

"You talked to his associates . . . of course."

Sykes nodded. "His parents, who hadn't seen him for over a year. His girl friend, who said she knew nothing about his employment, though judging from the style in which they were living Baker must have been pretty flush. A couple of his friends . . . you'd be surprised how much they didn't know, between them."

"So it has given you no idea whatsoever—"

"We're keeping an eye on the situation. That seems to be all we can do."

"Do you think if I—"

"I wouldn't recommend it, Mr. Maitland, really I wouldn't."

"Perhaps not, but if it gave me a lead—"

"Dolly Walters might be more forthcoming with someone unconnected with the police," said Sykes doubtfully.

"The girl friend? Tell me where I can find her."

"Buckingham House apartments, near Putney Heath. She's known as Mrs. Baker there."

"Is she—er—"

"She's honest enough, if that's what you mean. Seems to have been genuinely fond of Eddie." He shook his head sadly. "I can't see that it's going to help you, Mr. Maitland. I can't see it at all."

After that they were summoned because the kettle was boiling, and each abandoned the discussion thankfully enough. But Chief Inspector Sykes was unusually preoccupied for the rest of the day. He had cast his bread upon the waters, but he wasn't at all sure what the result would be.

IV

Roger came around that evening, after he had left Meg at the theater. He said they had been on a shopping spree, and he was seriously considering filing his petition in bankruptcy. Jenny, who still seemed to be out of spirits, told him he shouldn't joke about serious subjects, and went away and created a clatter in the kitchen, which was a thing she normally never did.

Neither of the men seemed to be much impressed by this display of energy. Roger said, "What was that in aid of?" and settled himself more comfortably in his chair. Antony went and sat on the sofa, and gave him a grin, but there was an undertone of anxiety in his voice when he replied.

"Lynn Edison. Have you heard what's happened?"

"Oh, yes, I've heard. At least three people rang Meg up to tell her. What's the score?"

"She didn't do it."

"You sound unusually sure of yourself."

"I am sure. She was enticed to the flat by a phone call. For some reason she still thinks it was genuine, but it seems obvious to me it was a fake."

"If that's your only reason—"

"It isn't. She says it was a flat voice . . . *I* think it was disguised. But when I made her repeat what had been said to her, it seemed obvious that the caller was an American."

"Why?"

"*He wants to talk* with *you* isn't conclusive, either way. But I never knew an Englishman to say, '*Is* this *Miss Edison speaking?*' "

"A bit tenuous, isn't it?"

"That's what the police would have said, so I didn't tell them. Besides, they didn't really believe in the telephone call. Now, she may have been indulging in an elaborate deception, but I don't think she's a good enough actress for that. So I thought at once—of course, as Lynn would say—of your friend Whitehead."

"Did you?" said Roger. He sounded startled, so that Antony was at once on the defensive.

"It isn't really so illogical. Granville owns the *Hazard Club*, which Whitehead frequents. . . . Granville is murdered, and an attempt made to implicate Lynn—"

"A pretty successful attempt."

"Yes . . . granted. But I don't think she was lying about the phone call, really I don't. So I don't think it's surprising I'm getting ideas in my head, do you?"

"No," said Roger in a reflective tone. And then, more positively, "I've given up being surprised at anything you do. And you needn't remind me it's Meg's fault . . . again. I'm only too well aware of it."

"I'd forgotten, as a matter of fact. Meg might be able to tell me—"

"You shouldn't encourage her, you know."

"No . . . really. About Granville's friends. And you needn't worry, you know, Roger. It's quite straightforward, this time."

"Including Eddie Baker, about whom you have so carefully refrained from reminding me?"

"Eddie Baker is dead."

"Yes, but—"

"Do you think you could find out anything for me about a chap called Vincent Lucas?"

"I'll try if you like, but why should you think—?"

"He's the manager of the Sloane Square branch of Bramley's Bank. You're one of their clients, aren't you?"

"A valued client, I daresay. That doesn't mean they'd encourage me to ask questions out of turn."

"I thought perhaps your brother-in-law . . . is he still at Fenchurch Street?"

"We do happen to be on speaking terms at the moment," said Roger doubtfully. And again, "I'll try if you like."

"Lucas is the witness I told you about."

"The one you saw at the *Hazard Club*. I don't think much of that."

"He was friendly enough with Granville, in spite of what he said. Still, as you say, what's a little matter of perjury between friends? I'd like to have seen him anyway, he ought to be able to tell me something about Granville . . . don't you think?"

"What about the other witnesses?"

"Not young Baird, the generation gap is too great. Besides, I doubt if he knows anything that isn't in the publicity handouts. Stevenson I should like to see, of course, but the thing is, I expect they'll all be called by the prosecution. To prove motive their evidence will have to be, to some extent, a repeat of that which was given in the libel case."

"And do you want to see Whitehead too?"

"That goes without saying."

"I don't like it, Antony."

"You're as bad as Inspector Sykes."

"Now look here, if Sykes is worried about the position—"

"It makes him uneasy, but he has no information to justify the feeling."

"What does he say about Whitehead, anyway?"

"That he's probably the front man for some very good, above suspicion, holier-than-thou racketeer 'back home.' At least, he didn't exactly say that, he allowed me to infer it."

"Well, then—"

"No, the only thing that worries me really is Johnny Lund. He's fallen in love with the girl, and I can't help feeling it complicates matters rather."

"I don't see why. He's young," said Roger heartlessly. "He'll get over it."

Jenny came back then, with the coffee pot, and Roger went to fetch the tray. She seemed to have forgiven them both, which Antony felt was unjust of her, but he let it go, and presently the talk turned to other things.

MONDAY, *4th March* ❧

I

The formality of winding up the libel action didn't take long on Monday morning, and Maitland was free by eleven o'clock to accept his uncle's invitation and look in at the court where the probate case was being heard. At the luncheon recess he waited in the corridor until Sir Nicholas came from the robing room. "Do you feel like eating?" he inquired sympathetically. "Or has it taken your appetite away?"

"I might toy with a little something, for the sake of my health," said the older man, falling into step beside him.

They went to Astroff's. "This Granville business," said Antony, when they were alone between courses. "Bellerby's will be sending you a brief. Do you mind?"

"After the present case . . . I thought Lynn Edison was your client."

"I shall have plenty to do in the background."

"I see." He managed to infuse a wealth of meaning into the words. "Will it come up for trial before Easter?"

"I think so. I hope so . . . in a way."

"What is the defense?"

"She denies it." Sir Nicholas snorted. "I believe her, as it happens."

"So you told me. Is that all you have to offer?"

"A fake telephone call—untraceable, of course—which Granville's manservant denies having made. I admit we've only Lynn's word for that, too."

"What else?"

"The murder weapon. A service revolver—Johnny's got the details—which anyone might have brought home as a souvenir after the war.'

"Is that all?"

"Absolutely all, so far. Except that he was shot at close range . . . about a foot, they say."

"So that even an inexperienced girl . . . I suppose I must accept the brief, if only to keep an eye on your activities."

"It will make a nice change. Lynn Edison is a good-looking lass."

"I don't usually choose my clients for their beauty," said Sir Nicholas, very repressively indeed. And then, "You've been seeing Chief Inspector Sykes again," he added suspiciously.

"To be exact, I've been picking his brains."

"Anything useful?"

"This and that." He saw the waiter coming, with a laden tray. "I can take it as settled then?"

"If it will make you any happier."

"It will make my day," Maitland told him. In spite of his light tone, it is a fact that he felt relieved. Perhaps it was merely the knowledge that he was committed now to Lynn Edison's defense, that he had burnt his boats.

II

The mood lasted until he got back to chambers, and was dissipated abruptly when he found Johnny Lund waiting for him in his room. One look was enough to tell him that Johnny's normal equilibrium had vanished as if it had never been. He was standing by the window when Maitland went in, but left it immediately and commenced to pace up and down in the narrow space between desk and bookcase. Antony went to his own chair, suppressing the instinct to prowl about the room which was his normal reaction to moments of stress. "What's the matter," he asked. "Did they spring some new evidence on you at the hearing?"

"Nothing like that. At least, it sounded bad enough, but we knew that anyway. Look here, she didn't do it, you've got to believe her."

"I had already reached that conclusion."

"Had you really? I thought—" Johnny stopped his pacing and stood at the corner of the desk. Maitland looked up at him inquiringly.

"I didn't realize you needed convincing," he said. "You'd better tell me what did the trick."

"I thought she'd done it, but I thought . . . well, Granville asked for it, didn't he?"

"I don't think I can follow you as far as that."

"Can't you? Well, it doesn't matter. She can't have done it . . . she thinks *I* did."

"*What*?"

"She thinks I did," Johnny repeated with gloomy emphasis. "I suppose—"

"Wait a bit. You'd better tell me—"

"Well, I suppose it was stupid of me, I did carry on about Granville rather. On Thursday night . . . I could already see how badly things were going."

"You said you'd like to murder him, I suppose," said Maitland, resigned.

"Something like that."

"Of all the idiotic—"

"Yes, I know. I know that now, but I never thought she'd

take me seriously. I suppose I must have given myself away to her . . . what I feel about her, I mean."

"Did she tell you . . . did she accuse you in so many words?"

"Not exactly. We were alone for a moment before the hearing, and she asked me where I'd been last night, and I told her I'd gone to the cinema, and she asked if I'd been alone, and I said 'Yes.' And then she said she hadn't told anybody about the threats I made, and she didn't mean to. Reassuringly, you know. It was easy enough to see what she meant, but damn it all, does she think I'd stand by and let her take the blame? And now I don't know what to do."

Maitland eyed him uneasily. "If you're thinking of confessing . . . don't."

"I wasn't thinking of that exactly," said Johnny, and immediately contradicted himself. "It seems the only way—"

"To put yourself right with Lynn? The thing's complicated enough already, without you making it worse."

"It isn't that I've any personal interest in her welfare," said Johnny, with a rather drastic reversal of attitude. "In fact," he added, more naturally, "I'd like to wring her neck."

"There you go again, you see. Will you never learn? Besides, you admit yourself you were convinced Lynn was guilty. I don't see that you can blame her for thinking the same thing about you."

"Oh . . . well! But don't you see that it puts me in an impossible situation."

"It's unusual, certainly," said Maitland, and let his mind dwell for a moment on Sir Nicholas's possible reaction, if he ever found out. "The only thing to do," he went on firmly, "is to get her acquitted first, and then worry about how to convince her—"

"But, can we? Get her acquitted, I mean."

"We can try. Sit down, Johnny, you're making me nervous, standing there. You'd better hear what I've been doing." He gave a brief outline of his talk with Sykes, and the request he had made to Roger Farrell.

"I don't quite see what you're getting at," said Johnny, when he had finished.

"I'm wondering if, perhaps, the Club isn't being used as a front for something less innocent than gambling."

"That wouldn't explain——"

"It might. And the idea of framing Lynn must have seemed an excellent one in the circumstances. This explains, by the way, why she was so certain the telephone call was genuine, not a fake."

"She thought I'd let her take the blame for me, but that I'd draw the line at setting a trap for her," said Johnny sourly. "Am I supposed to be grateful for that?"

It seemed better to ignore this. "What happened at the magistrate's court. Was there anything new?"

"Only the valet's evidence. We already knew he didn't make the phone call. Friday was his evening out—Friday, and all day on Sunday—and he'd gone to a friend's house to play poker."

"What time?"

"He left just before six-thirty. Granville was going out for a meal."

"Did he, I wonder?"

"Yes, he went down to the restaurant in the building at about seven o'clock."

"Rather early, wasn't it?"

"They say he'd left again before eight."

"Did the valet know of any appointment?"

"Not a thing. He may have been telling the truth," said Johnny doubtfully, "or he may have wanted to keep out of things as much as he could."

"I see. Well, the first thing to do is to see Anketell again, and then I want to get home early to have a word with Meg. Would you like to phone him from here?"

"Do you think he might be connected with the *Hazard Club?*"

"I've no reason to do so. He might be said to have a personal motive, though . . . if he came to believe that Granville murdered Cynthia Edison—"

"I don't see what could suddenly have convinced him of that."

"—or, on the other hand, if he thought Granville's behavior had brought her to a suicidal frame of mind."

"You can't very well ask him outright if he has an alibi," Johnny objected; he had his hand on the telephone, but made no immediate attempt to pick up the receiver.

"Well . . . hardly. I'll think of something, don't you worry," he added encouragingly. "Just give him a call and find out if he's in."

III

This time there was no question of delay. Antony got the impression as he passed that the waiting room was full of people, but the glamour girl smiled quite graciously and told them to go straight in. Anketell was occupied with a bulky volume of press cuttings, but he pushed it aside when he saw who the visitors were. Nothing seemed to ruffle his composure, thought Maitland, a little resentfully, though he must be able to guess. . . .

"I can guess what brought you here," said Anketell, as though in confirmation. "I don't see how I can help you, though."

"There is always the question of your evidence."

"*My* evidence?" Even with the emphasis he didn't exactly sound surprised. "I thought . . . the libel action is surely dead now."

"As dead as Granville. Yes, of course. But you've heard what's happened . . . haven't you?"

"If you mean that Lynn Edison has been arrested, I read the papers. . . . I could hardly have missed it. I don't see, though, what it has to do with me."

"Motive will be an integral part of the case for the prosecution. Won't it?" he added to Johnny, who nodded energetically. "If we can show it was non-existent—"

"I don't follow you, I'm afraid."

"Lynn was going to win her case, therefore she had no need to dispose of Granville."

"But . . . was she?"

Maitland smiled at him. "With your help," he insisted gently. "At any rate, that's what I shall tell the court. It follows, therefore—"

"I'm beginning to see."

"I'm sure you are. Now, you say you told Cynthia Edison about the part you wanted her to play in *The Silent City*. Can you bring any additional proof of that?"

"How could I?"

"If you'd mentioned your intention to your secretary, that would be something."

"I didn't."

"You sound very positive."

"Miss James is very discreet, but you know how things get about. I wanted this to be a surprise for Cynthia."

"You're going to be asked, you know, why there was nothing in writing."

"I told her on Friday afternoon. I meant to put the paperwork in hand the following Monday."

"Did you, in fact, start to do so, before you knew she was dead?"

"No, I didn't."

"When did you hear the news?"

"At lunch time, so far as I recollect. It was in the early edition of the *Evening Chronicle*."

(And that doesn't ring true, he's talking about the death of the girl he was in love with.) "So far as you recollect?" said Maitland inquiringly.

"No, I remember quite well now. That's how it was."

"You didn't regard the contract as very important, then."

"Of course not. Do you know a man called Lucas? Vincent Lucas."

"I'm sorry, darling. I don't."

He had no better luck when he questioned Roger on the same subject later in the evening. The brother-in-law who was a bank manager had been unable, or unwilling, to help him.

And when he went, the following morning, to Buckingham House, the so-called Mrs. Baker was no longer in residence. Nor had she left any forwarding address.

He put the problem to Sykes over the telephone, but the Chief Inspector declined to get excited over it. "Gone back to her own environment, I wouldn't wonder," he said prosaically. "I'll see what I can find out." But he added a warning before he rang off. "You'd do best to leave all this to me."

"The question is, how far are you prepared to take it? Will you tell Conway you think Granville's death was a gang killing?"

"I would, if I thought it was true."

"Let's get this straight. You think the *Hazard Club*—"

"If I'm right, it is operated with a strict regard for propriety."

"As a cover for something else."

"Well, yes."

"Then surely Granville's death—"

"There is not necessarily a connection. Quite frankly, Mr. Maitland, I find your client's story a bit too much to swallow."

"I see."

"That's why I'm counseling caution."

"You always do."

" 'appen you're right. But in this case you'd be exposing yourself to danger, without any corresponding benefit—"

"Why do you suppose Eddie Baker was killed?"

"Because he'd made an attempt on your life. Is that what you mean?"

"I've been wondering about that."

"You may be right. But I shouldn't count on continued immunity, if I were you."

All of which might be true. He glossed over this angle when he was speaking to Jenny, and did the best he could to undo the effects of his own imprudence. "Meg was quite right. I was only joking when I talked about the Mafia."

"I don't believe you," said Jenny, stabbing her needle into the slip she was shortening as though it had given her some personal cause of grievance.

"The tongue is an unruly evil," said Antony gloomily. "I ought to have had more sense."

Jenny glanced up at him. "It doesn't much matter what you say or don't say, Antony. I can always tell."

"When I'm going to make a fool of myself?"

"If you like to put it that way." He hoped she was smiling, but her head was bent over her work again, he couldn't see her eyes. "The only thing is, I sometimes wonder . . . why?"

"Jenny love, I'm worried to death about Lynn Edison. That's what you wanted, isn't it? You and Meg."

"There hadn't been a murder then."

"But—don't you see?—that's what makes it so important. It's bad enough putting people in prison when they've done something, that can't be helped. But since I'm sure she's innocent—" He broke off, with a helpless gesture. Jenny was intent upon her sewing.

"Besides," she said, "there's Johnny to think of, isn't there?"

"He's a young fool," said Antony crossly. But when it came to the point he couldn't have denied it . . . he did feel responsible.

The fact that the feeling was completely illogical was no help at all.

THURSDAY, *7th March*

The prosecution case, as revealed to Johnny Lund, was developing just as he would have expected. The libel action would be the crux of the matter, as showing motive, and the three witnesses as to damage would be called, as before. This left him without a line of approach, except through Oscar Whitehead and the *Hazard Club*, though he was still interested in Vincent Lucas and had set Johnny Lund to finding out more about him if he could, through that reputable and discreet firm of inquiry agents, Cobbold's. Mr. Bellerby, the senior partner, consulted as a matter of courtesy, shook his head in a foreboding way, but he was on the whole inclined to be a partisan of Maitland's, and to let him have his head.

A date to revisit the club was fixed with Roger for the end of the week, and life fell back into its normal absorbing routine again. But that was before Mrs. Walters came into his life.

She arrived in chambers late on Thursday afternoon, a dumpy little woman wearing a bright red coat with fur at the collar, and a green woollen headscarf. Her round face was rosy, and fell normally into cheerful lines, though by the time she reached Maitland's room she was inclined to be ruffled, probably by old Mr. Mallory's ineffable air of condescension. But her smile came back as she sank down into the visitor's chair.

"You'd be the chap as was looking for our Dolly?"

"Yes. Mrs. Walters—"

"Mrs. Dorothea Walters, seeing as I'm a widow."

"Yes, of course," said Maitland vaguely. "I was hoping for a word with Mrs. Baker—"

He wasn't destined to finish that sentence either. "Now, that's something I don't hold with, young man."

"Er . . . what—?"

"Deceitfulness," said Mrs. Walters severely. "Not calling a thing by its proper name. Dolly Walters she was born, and Dolly Walters she still is, to my certain knowledge."

"I . . . see."

"That's all right then. Not that I wouldn't have liked to see her wed, legal, and her so fond of Eddie. But 'I can hold him, Mum,' she said to me, 'marriage lines or no.' And so she would have done if he hadn't got himself shot."

"Yes, of course," said Antony, this time in sincere agreement. If the girl took after her mother. . . .

"Well, I went to see Fred Parsons when I knew she wasn't at the flat any longer. He's the janitor there, and he give me your card. So I said to myself I'd better find out what he's wanting, because it might be something to her advantage, as they say, and I wouldn't want Dolly to miss anything like that."

"I'm afraid . . . I wanted her to help me, if she would."

"Well, there now! I'm sure Dolly would have done anything. Too good-natured for her own good, and so I've often told her."

"You don't know where she is?"

"No, I don't. And if you want to know I've been fair narked about it, what with the police asking questions, and all. But she'll turn up again one of these days. For one thing, she left clothes and such at the flat."

"Did she, though?"

"Dolly isn't one to let things go like that. Brought up careful, she was, not to be wasteful. Besides, she's fond of me, for all I've always spoke my mind."

"Mrs. Walters, do you think you can help me?"

That stopped her for a moment. "How?" she asked, and looked almost wary.

"By telling me what you know of Eddie Baker."

"Oh . . . him! He wasn't good enough for Dolly, I can tell you that."

"Was he an excitable sort of chap . . . impulsive?"

She showed no sign of finding the question an odd one. "Well, I don't see why I should help you, but then again, I don't see why I shouldn't. He was and he wasn't," she said.

"You're going to have to explain that to me, I'm afraid," said Maitland, and smiled at her. To his relief, she returned the smile, though her voice was lugubrious when she replied.

"He was easy-going where Dolly was concerned. Anything she wanted . . . she'd tell you that. But he'd the devil's own pride, and that's a fact. If he thought anyone was trying to get at him, he'd flare up in a minute. I told Dolly there'd be trouble come of that some day, but she was bound to have her own way."

"What was his occupation?"

"I only know what Dolly told me . . . *he* liked to be mysterious. Hints about big deals, and that. I didn't trust him, and that's a fact."

"But your daughter told you—?"

"She said he used to drive for a gentleman, which I told her straight didn't sound like much of a job, and him so set up with himself. But she said the money was good, and why should she care if Eddie liked to pretend to be important?"

"Do you think—forgive me, Mrs. Walters—do you think she was telling you the truth?"

She sat looking at him then, and for the first time her eyes were troubled. "If something was wrong, my Dolly didn't know about it." He did not reply, just nodded his head as though in agreement, and after a moment she went on. "Well, I did think she'd told me just to shut me up, you know, to stop me asking questions. But whether it was true or not . . . they *did* seem to be rather flush."

"Did she say who he was working for?"

"She did. And that's a funny thing, now, isn't it? It was that Paul Granville as got himself shot the other day."

"Paul Granville!"

"You must have heard of him. A big star, he was. That's what made me wonder, you see, if Dolly was telling the truth, or just putting on airs."

"Mrs. Walters, you remember when Eddie Baker was killed?" He was eager now, and she seemed to take alarm from his eagerness.

"Of course I do," she told him, but her tone had its reservations.

"I just wondered—" He sat back in his chair, and with an effort achieved a casual air. "I just wondered whether she said anything that might explain . . . that might make you think she knew—"

"She didn't know why he'd been killed, if that's what you mean."

"Are you sure?"

"I'm telling you, aren't I?"

"You yourself—?"

"And if I did, there's some things best not talked of."

He didn't leave it there, of course, but she was cautious now, and he didn't get any more information.

He grabbed the telephone as soon as she had gone, and thought himself lucky to have caught Johnny Lund before he left the office. "Had Paul Granville a car?"

"Yes, a Mercedes. He didn't use it in town, though."

"No chauffeur, then?"

"If you'd read the stuff I sent you—"

"I'm sorry, I've been busy." As an apology it was perfunctory, and not altogether honest. "Did he have a chauffeur?"

"No. He used a car belonging to the *Hazard Club* sometimes."

"Well, now!" He sounded pleased, and Johnny's tone became correspondingly gloomy.

"I don't see where that gets us."

"Did he drive himself?"

"He didn't like driving in town."

"Who drove him, then?"

"One of the Club employees, I suppose. I don't exactly know."

"Find out, will you?"

"Anything you say." He sounded resigned rather than enthusiastic, and Maitland said, answering the tone rather than the words, "What's up?"

"I think you're barking up the wrong tree."

"I should have thought you'd want to try everything."

"Yes, but . . . if you haven't read what I sent you, you don't know anything about Granville's will."

"Tell me."

"Everything to Danny Owen."

This seemed unreasonable to Antony, and he said so. "Hadn't he any relations?"

"No one, apparently. All the same—"

"Owen might not have been arriving at Granville's flat for the first time when he found Lynn there. Is that what you're thinking?"

"If you're not interested—"

"Of course I'm interested," said Maitland, with some exasperation evident in his tone. "Have you asked Cobbold's to look into Danny Owen for us? And to find out whether he had an alibi."

"He couldn't have had. He was there too."

"No, but if he'd been with somebody the time element might

work in his favor . . . or not. What have they to say about Oscar Whitehead?"

"Nothing so far."

"What about Vincent Lucas?"

"All that's come out of that inquiry is that he's living at Leinster Court."

"And Tom Thorne?"

"He took Lynn out once or twice over a year ago. She threw him over for Granville, I suppose, but I don't imagine he's been brooding on the fact ever since, and planning his revenge," said Johnny sarcastically.

"You're quite right, of course, it doesn't seem likely."

"If you concentrated on Anketell there'd be more sense to it. He was prevaricating at one point when you talked to him, wasn't he?"

"I'm inclined to believe him. Some people just don't like answering questions." He hesitated. "You realize that Danny Owen owns the *Hazard Club* now?"

"Considering that I told you—"

"So you did."

"But he could have killed Granville for what he had to leave, without all this complication about the Club's hidden activities," said Johnny. "I don't believe it's relevant."

"That's what Sykes says," agreed Antony, depressed.

And that was how matters stood when he phoned Sykes the following morning. But he nearly forgot the information he had been about to impart when the Chief Inspector told him that Dolly Walters had been found.

FRIDAY, *8th March*

I

There are six cashiers at the Cannongate branch of Bramley's Bank, and on Friday mornings each one has his float substantially increased, in preparation for a busy day. That Friday morning—Friday, the eighth of March—was no different from any other, except that the sun had come out, giving some promise of a fine weekend.

Freda Jameson hadn't been on the counter for long. She took her responsibilities seriously, checking the contents of her drawer meticulously when it was brought from the strong room, making sure that her supply of check books was equal to any reasonable demands. This care was all the more commendable because she was intensely interested in the man at the next wicket, Timothy Aspinall, who played rugger for the bank, and who had slammed his own drawer cheerfully into place with the insouciance of one in a privileged position, for whom "overs and shorts in cash" presented no terrors. He didn't return Freda's interest . . . she was the sort of nice girl who might well be somebody's sister; but he was quite ready to enter into a conversation about anything, or nothing, as a way of passing the time. Griffiths, the messenger, had only just unlocked the heavy doors, and it wasn't likely that the first customers were actually queueing up on the pavement outside.

A quarter of an hour later, however, they were all busy, except Griffiths, who was loitering impressively in his uniform. Mr. Tomlinson, the chief cashier, who was reputed to have the signature of every one of the branch's customers indelibly recorded in his memory, was counting up a sizeable deposit from one of the neighboring offices, while Freda, at the till nearest the accountant's desk, was cashing a check for a very deaf old lady, and finding it difficult to make herself heard. It was as the old lady, who needed reassuring every week that her account was in safe keeping, was scooping seven pound notes and six ten shillings into her handbag, that the door was pushed open again and four masked men came in, three of them armed. The fourth man closed the door carefully, and slid across the heavy bolts.

Freda's first thought was one of stunned disbelief. The masks gave the whole thing an air of unreality. Someone was shooting a film, and the staff hadn't been told about it. And the way the four men behaved, as though they had been drilled in every detail, might have lent color to this belief if the leader's first action had not been, quite deliberately and cold-bloodedly, to fire at Griffiths. The messenger was knocked backward by the force of the shot, then he fell, slowly, like a marionette when the guiding hand is taken away. The three supporting players came up alongside the leader, and fanned out beside him.

"Back! Get back! Hands on your heads where I can see them. Anybody can have what this guy got," said the leader harshly, and kicked as he spoke at Griffiths, who now lay ominously still. Freda backed away instinctively, and sensed as she did so that her colleagues were following suit; even Mr. Tomlinson, who had what they all called the "panic button," but there'd been no time to think of that. The customers strained back against the counter; only the old lady, who had heard none of this, stood staring in bewilderment at Freda's unexpected movement, and then turned around to see what the girl was gaping at. The shot carried her back against the counter before she fell, as slackly as the bank messenger had done.

There was no arguing after that.

II

And so it came about that at four o'clock that afternoon Chief Inspector Sykes was in the Divisional Detective Inspector's office at Faraday Street. There had been murder done, as well as larceny, and the job, besides, was one of a series, not all of which had taken place in the same division. "It was slick, all right," the D.D.I. was saying. "Like a well-oiled machine," he added, without much originality, and sighed.

"It sounds like the same people," said Sykes in his placid way. He was regretting his own orderly room at New Scotland Yard; this one was dusty, and untidy, and smelled of stale cigarette smoke. "Unless there was deliberate copying of the method, the newspapers will go into details. But that doesn't seem likely, it would mean a second gang as ruthless as the first."

"So it would," said the D.D.I. sadly.

"If you don't mind just running over it once more."

"Glad to, if it will help matters." (He didn't sound glad.) "Nine customers in bank, day's business just getting under way. Four men come in, shutting and locking the door behind them. Stocking masks, must have pulled them on in the lobby. Tall man, seems to be leader, shoots messenger. No apparent reason, fellow was just standing there. Three of them have sawn-off shotguns, nasty mess."

"Untidy," Sykes agreed.

"Then they gave the usual orders, hands on heads, customers backed up against the counter, cashiers backed away from it.

The old lady took no notice; cashier says she's deaf. Anyway, they shot her too. This time none of the witnesses can agree which of the men fired the shot. Two men go behind, past the securities desk, obviously had looked the place over beforehand. One with gun, one with sack, easy matter to empty the tills. Accountant told to open up strong room; one of the clerks had the other key, of course. Sensible man, didn't argue. Got away with about two hundred thousand pounds all told."

"And two completely gratuitous murders," Sykes said thoughtfully.

"It's all part of the pattern, isn't it? But they didn't have to shoot the old lady." The D.D.I. sounded resentful. "Three men walked to the car, taking their time. The other held the rear, locked the door, and then made a run for it. Getaway car a Rover 2000."

"That's the same make they've used for the last two jobs," Sykes put in.

"Is that so? One stolen from Palace Court was found abandoned in Brenton Street half an hour ago. Of course, it may not be the same one."

"I expect it is."

"Yes, I daresay. They'd removed their masks, of course, weren't seen in them in the street. Manager in his room throughout the whole affair, never heard a thing."

"Then there's the other old lady," said Sykes in an encouraging tone.

"That's right. She lives in Brenton Street, and she was looking out of her window, and she saw five men get out of one car and into another, exactly similar except for the color. She thought it was funny, and that's all she thought about it until our chaps started asking questions. No idea of the number, of course, but your people are looking through records, seeing if any of our regulars owns a dark green Rover. You never know, it may pay off, though I wouldn't trust her to be right about the two cars being the same."

While he was still speaking, the telephone rang.

III

Antony told Roger about his talk with Sykes when Farrell came in that evening, as he so often did after leaving Meg at the theater. They were going to the *Hazard Club,* but it was too early to start yet. Jenny had taken herself to the pictures, and Maitland thought it was because she was worried, but at least she hadn't said anything. "Things are beginning to move," he told his friend glumly.

"That ought to please you."

"In a negative and non-helpful way." He paused and kicked the fire, which seemed to be feeling sulky, and added, still looking down at it, "You remember I was looking for Eddie Baker's girl friend?"

"Yes."

"She's been found."

"Isn't that a good thing?" asked Roger cautiously.

"They fished her out of the river."

"Dead?"

"Yes, of course. She'd been there the best part of a week, the doctor says."

"Was it suicide?"

"She'd been shot."

"Where?"

"Through the head. Oh, I see, you mean *where*? Nothing to show where the event took place." He looked round then, and said with more energy, "I'll tell you one thing. The police haven't finished their tests yet, but they think it was the same gun that killed Eddie Baker."

"Well, I suppose . . . you say Sykes told you all this."

"He did. I don't expect they'd have got around to identifying her so quickly if he hadn't been looking out for the girl."

"What does it mean . . . that she knew something?"

"Something that connected Eddie with the *Hazard Club,* at a guess."

"Does Sykes agree with you?"

"Not exactly. I mean, he does as far as that, and what Mrs. Walters told me yesterday tends to confirm it. But he thinks I'm deceiving myself in thinking that it has anything to do with Lynn Edison's affairs."

Roger thought about that for a moment. "He may be right," he said.

"Don't I know it. Even Johnny thinks I'm mistaken, though *he* believes in Lynn's innocence, which I suppose is something. And I hardly dare discuss the matter with Uncle Nick."

"Does he disagree with you too?"

"I'd rather not give him a chance to. Did I tell you that Danny Owen is Paul Granville's sole heir?"

"Is he?"

"Under a will made a year ago. And if you want to know why I mention that fact, it's because Whitehead told us he has been in England for twelve months now."

"I don't see—"

"Gossip says it was about a year ago that Granville paid off his mortgage."

"You think Whitehead paid it?"

"I'm guessing, you don't have to remind me of that. If he did —on behalf of his principal in the States, I suppose—he might also have suggested to Granville that a will should be made in favor of someone who, in his turn, would be a good tool."

"Which reminds me . . . you haven't seen the paper this evening?"

"Not yet. Is there something—?" There was a copy of the *Evening Chronicle* on the sofa, and he bent down to pick it up. "I see what you mean," he said after a moment, studying the glaring headlines. "Another bank robbery."

"And two more deaths. Do you think—?"

"Assuming they're all done by the same gang . . . well, we think Eddie Baker drove for them on at least one occasion, and we've been told he sometimes drove Paul Granville. Even Sykes admits the connection there."

"I see. We've come a long way from Cynthia Edison and the overdose of *Drowse*, haven't we?"

"We have, rather. I'm beginning to wonder whether Granville killed her, after all."

"Did she commit suicide then?"

"I don't think so. I was wondering, perhaps, if one of the gang—"

"Why should they want her out of the way. You'll be telling me next that she knew to much."

"I think very likely she did, poor girl. Don't you see, if Granville let slip something by mistake, that might be an additional reason for them wanting him out of the way."

"Additional to what?"

"I was asking him about the *Hazard Club*, and my questions made him uneasy. For all they knew, I should have returned to the subject in court on Monday morning. If they didn't trust him—"

"Wouldn't that have been a little drastic?"

"Come now, that's the one thing we're sure of about these people . . . that they're ruthless."

"I still think it's more likely, if Cynthia was murdered, that Granville did it himself. I mean, it would have to be someone she knew quite well."

"So it would. Or perhaps she was part of the gang too, and—"

"Does it matter?"

"Not really. Not now. But I confess I'd like to know the answer."

They talked of other things then, until it was time to leave. Roger had his car, and they picked up the obliging Mr. Carpenter, who was again going to sponsor them, on the way. They were late enough for the club to have warmed up nicely. "It looks like a gold mine," said Antony, as they lingered in the hall.

"I expect they get by," commented Roger dryly, and made

129

for the larger of the salons, and one of the roulette tables, as they had previously arranged.

Left to himself, Maitland wandered. He found Oscar Whitehead in the baccarat room, and came up quietly to his elbow. "Still observing?" he asked.

If Whitehead was startled, he didn't show it. He turned, smiling, and then gesticulated toward the door, and the hall beyond. "I might ask you the same thing," he said, when they were out of earshot of the players.

"Why, yes, of course. I have an interest, you know, in anything to do with Paul Granville."

"Even now he's dead?"

"Because he's dead."

"And that silly little girl is your client."

"If you mean Lynn Edison, not any longer, though I'm helping to prepare the defense. But it's a very poor description."

"From what I've seen in the papers—"

"You shouldn't believe all you read. Now, I've heard Mr. Owen is the new owner here. Can you tell me if that is true?"

"Yes, I believe it is."

"Has he told you when he expects the accountants to come in?"

"The . . . accountants."

"The Club will have to be evaluated for estate duty."

"Naturally. But I can't imagine that they will discover anything of interest to you. From what I have . . . observed, it is such a well run place," said Whitehead smoothly.

"Yes, I'm sure of that. Do you know most of the Club servants?"

"I think so, by now."

"I'm interested in a chap called Eddie Baker."

"Eddie Baker? I don't think—"

"He's dead, too," said Maitland helpfully.

"Then I don't quite see—"

"He was shot in the back . . . oddly enough, on the night of our first meeting."

"The murder on the demolition site? I remember reading about it, of course, but I'm sure Granville would have told me if there'd been any connection with the club."

"Baker used to drive for Granville sometimes . . . or so I've been told."

"I wonder who told you that." Whitehead's tone remained casual, but his shaggy eyebrows came together in a frown.

"A girl called Dolly. I'm not sure whether she was Baker's wife or not." That seemed the safest thing to say; at least, it could no longer do Dolly Walters any harm.

"In any case, the information was hardly of earth-shaking importance."

"No, it wasn't, was it? It's a good thing I talked to her, though."

There was a moment's silence. Then Whitehead said, as though he couldn't help himself, "Why is that?"

"Because she's dead too, poor girl."

"Not another victim of violence?"

"I'm afraid she was."

"I shall be getting nervous myself. The casualty rate among your acquaintances seems rather high."

"I don't think you need worry." He paused a moment, weighing his next words. "Mr. Lucas doesn't seem to be here tonight."

"Mr. Lucas?"

"Don't you know him? Vincent Lucas. I saw him when I was here before."

"Now I remember. He isn't a regular visitor. And he would tell you, I am sure, that he only came once, out of interest in a client's affairs."

"Because of his position in the bank, you mean? I don't suppose gambling is exactly favored by Head Office as a hobby."

"He only came once," said Whitehead again. "I don't think he played at all."

"I see." He let the silence grow between them. "I hear you're a member of my own profession, in the States."

"Who told you that?"

"Someone or other," said Maitland, and gestured vaguely. "I forget."

"Why did you come here tonight? Were you looking for me?" The questions came abruptly, and Whitehead was frowning again.

"Why should you think that? I came to watch Farrell play roulette, but the spectacle palled rather quickly. I like the atmosphere of the baccarat room better."

"You've had a wasted evening, I'm afraid. Don't you feel like taking a hand yourself?"

"I'm afraid my luck wouldn't hold. I'm more interested in a drink at the moment. Won't you join me?"

"Later, perhaps." But though Maitland lingered in the refreshment room for some time, until Roger came to find him, he did not see Whitehead again.

Roger was pleased with himself. "It seems churlish to retire when you're winning," he said, as they went down the steps, "but I thought you might be getting impatient."

"I was ready to leave."

"Did you see Whitehead? He was playing roulette for the past hour."

"Is that where he'd got to? I saw him before that. He is not completely unshakable, but I can't say I got much out of our talk. For one thing, I don't think he really likes me."

"One way and another, I'm not surprised."

"He denies any knowledge of Eddie Baker. I wonder what Danny Owen would say to a similar question."

"I haven't a clue. I saw him and had a word with him, but I kept it strictly noncommittal, as we agreed."

"How is he?"

"Rattled."

"That's good." They had reached the car now, and he got in and stretched out his legs luxuriously. "Altogether," he said, "I'm not ill-satisfied with the evening's work."

Roger got in too, and closed the door with a slam. "I don't see what you've got to be so pleased about."

"Don't you?"

"If you ask me, you've lighted the fuse and may expect an explosion at any moment."

"Precisely. But you must see, Roger, I'm not going to get anywhere unless I can provoke some action."

Roger, who was not given to displays of temper, started the car as smoothly as ever. "Is it so important?" he asked, after a moment.

"I think it is."

"They've abolished capital punishment."

"I hadn't forgotten. Can you honestly say you'd rather be put in prison for life?"

"You might get her off without—"

"Without providing an alternative suspect. Uncle Nick might . . . it's his case, remember? But I can't say that in the circumstances I think very much of his chances."

"Well, watch out, that's all."

"I shall be discretion itself."

IV

It was late when they got back to Kempenfeldt Square. Jenny would be home long since, and even Meg would have got back from the theater a couple of hours ago. Antony did not notice anyone as they drew up, but when he had said "Good night" and watched Roger drive off a man materialized suddenly out of the shadows. The odd thing about him was that he was carrying a gun, and he stood squarely between Maitland and the bottom of the steps to number five. Antony might have spoken airily about provoking some action, but he had hardly expected it to be as quick as this. Besides which, Roger had said that Whitehead was occupied at the roulette table. . . .

"If this is a hold-up," he said, "I'm afraid I've nothing on me to make it worth your while."

"Quiet!" said the man with the gun, tersely. And then, in apparent contradiction, "I want to talk to you."

"I am open for being talked to," said Maitland, "at this time of year." It wasn't any good trying to see the man's face; his hat was pulled well over his eyes, and a heavy scarf covered his mouth. "But it can't be good for you, out in the night air."

"It's what's good for you you should be thinking about," his companion told him grimly.

"Yes, but *I* haven't got a toothache," Antony pointed out.

"What? Oh, I see. Funny!" The muzzle of the gun was jammed hard into Maitland's side.

"You do know what would happen—don't you?—if that thing went off."

"I know all right."

"Well, if you really want me to concentrate on what you're going to say, you'll stand a little farther away." He moved casually as he spoke, and the man with the gun laughed.

"Nervous?" he said, and obligingly took a step backward. And as he did so, a car turned into the square from Avery Street, going rather fast. And, just for an instant, the gunman's eyes flickered, and as they did so Antony moved.

He brought his left hand up to catch his opponent under the wrist with a force that sent the automatic spinning, and while he was still off-balance brought him down by the simple, if inelegant, expedient of hooking a leg around his and tripping him. Then he brought his left hand down viciously on the back of the man's neck just as he was scrambling to his feet again.

For the moment the gunman lost all interest in the proceedings.

Maitland found the gun, and was interested to note that the safety catch was still in position, which meant, presumably, that the chap really had wanted to talk. Then he went indoors to use the telephone in Sir Nicholas's study. When he came back he found that his uncle had come downstairs in his dressing gown, and was peering distastefully down the steps at the man who lay there. "This passion of yours for brawling in the streets," he said fretfully. And the, "Er . . . is he dead?"

"Not he." He looked with interest around the silent square. "Nobody else seems to have heard us," he said.

"I was roused by the sound of your voices, right under my window. Otherwise you were reasonably silent. Have you called the police?"

"Naturally."

"And what are you going to tell them when they come?"

Antony grinned. "He wanted to talk to me," he said.

"A strange desire, but not one that would necessarily lead to violence." He descended the steps and took a closer look at the gunman. "Did you have to use such rough and ready methods?" he complained.

"You see," said Antony, "*I* didn't want to talk to him."

"So I suppose. Now, which of your friends—?"

"I haven't the faintest idea."

Sir Nicholas looked up at him. "I find that hard to believe," he remarked gently.

"You don't like my guesses, Uncle Nick."

"Am I right in thinking that he is connected in some way with Miss Edison's affairs?"

"I think so, but nobody seems to believe me."

"That seems a straightforward enough affair."

"I was afraid you'd say that. She didn't kill Granville, sir."

"Even granting that as a fact—for the sake of argument only —it hardly seems necessary to drag in the—the underworld."

"If they're already—" He broke off as another car turned into the square from Avery Street. "Here come the police."

"So I see." Sir Nicholas moved back to the steps again in a leisurely way. "My ankles are getting cold, I shall leave you to your explanations." He paused and laid a hand for a moment on his nephew's arm. "We must have a good talk about Miss Edison's affairs, my dear boy. Tomorrow, perhaps?" he suggested, and passed into the house.

V

Jenny was sitting up waiting for him. The room was warm, but the fire was nearly dead. "I don't suppose you need any more to drink," she said—it was a statement of fact, made without ulterior motive—"but would you like some tea?"

He followed her into the kitchen, where the kettle was already simmering. "Why aren't you in bed?"

"I had a message for you. You're very late, Antony."

"A slight *contretemps*. Nothing to worry about."

"Of course not." She was taking cups from the cupboard, and did not turn around as she spoke.

"Well, it isn't. What was the message, love?"

She hesitated a moment, and then turned to face him. "I'm sorry, Antony, it's Inspector Sykes—"

"Chief Inspector," he corrected her mechanically.

"—he's been shot, and he's in the hospital, and he's asking for you."

SATURDAY, *9th March*

I

He rang the hospital at once, of course, but got little satisfaction. The patient was "resting quietly"—which might, in his experience, mean anything or nothing—and most certainly could *not* be disturbed at that hour of the night.

It was therefore with considerable trepidation that he presented himself at the hospital next morning, to be greeted with starchy disapproval by the sister on duty. However, she had evidently resigned herself to permitting this one visitor at least, and once he had given the usual undertakings (he had no desire to stay longer than was necessary, and how would you set about exciting Sykes anyway?) there was no further delay in sending him up to one of the private rooms on the fifth floor.

The Chief Inspector was propped up on his pillows. The top part of his body was heavily bandaged, but his right arm was free, and it wasn't apparent that his placidity had been ruffled at all. He was, if anything, rather more Yorkshire than usual, both in mood and in speech.

"Well, now, Mr. Maitland," he said by way of greeting, "I'm obliged to you for coming so soon."

"I'm sorry you've been hurt, but I'm glad to see you looking so lively. The way they clammed up on me, I thought you were dead."

"Not this time."

"What happened?"

"It were nowt." He thought about this for a moment, perhaps wondering whether this obviously inaccurate statement could be left to stand alone. "You'll have read about the bank robbery yesterday," he said, after a while.

"The papers gave it rather a prominent display." He pulled up a chair as he spoke, and sat down, his eyes fixed on Sykes's face. "They said this morning that two men have been detained."

"So they have, but not without some difficulty."

"I gathered as much. How did you get on to them so quickly?"

"By chance. An old lady saw the robbers changing cars—she didn't know who they were, of course, but the incident stuck in her mind. And she didn't look at the number plate of the car they drove off in, but she did think it was the same make as the one they'd abandoned, which was a Rover 2000. So we got Records on to it, and they came up with Tiny Williams, who owns a 1965 model, and it wasn't maligning him too much to think he might have been driving the getaway car, and the local people knew where he lived, so we went to look him up."

That was a long speech for Sykes. Antony began to wonder what was coming next. He said, however, because he was curious, "You can't leave it there. How did that situation turn to violence?"

"You're right, it should have been merely a matter of a few questions at that stage. But knowing what had happened at the bank we weren't taking any chances, I can tell you."

"I can see you weren't," said Maitland, his eyes on the bandages.

"No avoidable risks," Sykes agreed amiably.

"Well? What happened?"

"Just a matter of routine, Mr. Maitland, as you might say," said Sykes with maddening deliberation. "Two men to watch the back door, three of us to the front. Woman who let us in told us that Williams was her lodger, and where his room was . . . on the left at the top of the stairs."

"So you went up?"

"We weren't looking for trouble, you know. Just a quiet chat, that's all we wanted. I took the local sergeant with me, a stiffish sort of chap, he is. We knocked, of course, and there was a bit of chit-chat back and forth, but the door was locked and they wouldn't open it."

"They?"

"Turned out he had a friend with him, name of Hall, but we didn't know that at the time. All we knew was, there were two of them, we could hear them whispering together, and then we heard a sort of a click . . . well, the thing was, Mr. Maitland, it sounded for all the world like a gun being cocked."

"And so it was, of course."

"As it turned out. But that sort of thing is alarming, you know," said Sykes mildly. "We took the door at a run, the sergeant and I . . . he's a heavier man than I am by two stones at least, I should say. And the lock gave, and the hinges, and we sprawled on top of it, but luckily Tiny Williams was safe underneath, though I don't think he found it comfortable."

"I don't suppose he did."

"A mass of bruises he'll be, I wouldn't wonder. But the other chap was clear of the scrum, you see, and it was he who had the gun, and he plugged me just as I got to my feet again."

"Were there any other casualties?"

"No." Sykes's smile had all its usual serenity. "By some happy chance when I fell down again I fell on top of Hall, and the sergeant's a quick man for all his size, he grabbed the gun before either of them got their breath back. That was all, really, but I didn't ask you here to tell you that."

"I don't suppose you did."

"I thought you might be willing—in the circumstances, you know—to give us a bit of help with our inquiries."

"Tell me first, has any of the loot been recovered?"

"Not a thing."

"How disappointing for you. All right, Chief Inspector, how can I help you?"

"By telling me what you know."

"I don't understand you. I was under the impression that I had been extremely frank."

"Up to a point, Mr. Maitland, up to a point."

"The only thing I haven't told you is what happened last night. And if you can make sense of it, it's more than I can do," he added reflectively.

"What happened last night?"

"I was held up in the square. No—wait a minute!—I'd been to the *Hazard Club* again, but if you're going to tell me it was cause and effect you're forgetting Eddie Baker."

"You mean Eddie was killed for being too impetuous."

"It looked like that, didn't it? But in that case, why the quick follow-up last night? I haven't an idea what the chap was after, the safety catch was still on the automatic, so it doesn't look as if his intentions were lethal. The police had arrived by the time he came around again, but from all the signs I don't think he was going to confide in them."

Sykes was looking amused. "A warning, I suppose. I gather you treated him roughly, which wasn't very grateful of you. What did you find at the *Hazard Club*?"

"That Danny Owen looks worried by his new responsibilities. That Oscar Whitehead is still in England, and disclaims any knowledge of Eddie Baker. Oh, yes, and that Roger's luck was in." He spread his hands as he spoke. "That's all, Chief Inspector. Nothing up my sleeve."

"There are two things I want to know," said Sykes, considering these facts and discarding them as irrelevant. "Why are you sure of Lynn Edison's innocence, and why do you think

Paul Granville's death is tied in in some way with the activities —if any—of the Club?"

"As for the first, I don't think you can expect me to tell you. It's a very small point, and could be made so much more effectively in court . . . if we find anything to back it up. As for the reason I suspect the Club's affairs to be in some way concerned . . . I don't trust Whitehead, and I don't—you see, it comes around full circle—I don't think Lynn is guilty."

"There must be more to it than that."

"N-nothing at all."

"Instinct, I daresay," said Sykes, deliberately ignoring the slight, angry stammer in his visitor's voice.

"It's quite l-logical, if you th-think about it."

"Now, it seems to me that Miss Edison's feud with Paul Granville is something quite apart from his connection with the Club."

"Yes, b-but I'm working from the f-fact of her innocence; don't you see?"

"I see you're not going to tell me."

"Oh, w-what's the use?" He got up as he spoke, and stood gazing down at Sykes, who still had his imperturbable look.

"I'm trying to persuade you, Mr. Maitland, that if the Mafia are trying to get a foothold in this country, which I think is very likely, it's our business, not yours. I also think . . . you may have trouble with Chief Inspector Conway, you know. He doesn't like interference."

"It's my b-business who k-killed Paul Granville." He stopped a moment, and then spoke more carefully. "I'm sorry you're laid up, but you shouldn't indulge in heroics, you know." (He could think of nothing more likely to annoy the detective than that.)

"I never—"

"What else do you call tackling a man with a gun? I'm sorry, too, that I can't help you. You'll just have to take my word for it that I don't know anything more."

But he was smiling to himself as he left the hospital a few

minutes later. He hadn't excited the patient, but he couldn't say the patient hadn't succeeded in exciting him.

II

On Saturdays Antony and Jenny generally lunched with Sir Nicholas, and were doing so today, so there was no hope at all of avoiding a meeting. His uncle waited only until the three of them were alone together before starting his questions. "Concerning the Edison brief, I want to know precisely what you're giving me to take into court."

"The prosecution will say Lynn killed Granville because he was going to win the libel action; we shall say she had no reason to kill him, because *she* was going to win."

"And shall we be believed?"

"I doubt it."

"In effect it will be the trial of the libel action over again."

"That's right. Our only witness, except Lynn herself, will be William Anketell, who will say that he told Cynthia Edison that the part she coveted was hers. As far as the murder charge is concerned, we have no evidence at all in refutation."

"I suspected as much," said Sir Nicholas in the meditative tone that generally spelled trouble. And then, "These other inquiries you are pursuing—?"

"Are leading to nothing . . . except a blank wall. The police are willing to concede that Granville was probably engaged in some illegal activity, for which the club provided a front— . . . at least, Sykes is, I don't know whether Conway would go as far as that. But they've no proof, even of that, and they still think Lynn Edison killed him."

"Being reasonable men," Sir Nicholas pointed out gently.

"You don't agree with me, sir?"

"Did you expect me to?"

"Since you ask me, no."

"How is Inspector Sykes?" asked Jenny, coming out of her silence.

"As well as can be expected." He hesitated. "Irrational," he said.

"That sounds very unlike him."

"He thinks I know something, Uncle Nick. I wish he was right."

"In the circumstances I must share your desire. The court, for instance, will not be interested in your—er—your private brawls," said Sir Nicholas crushingly.

"If I could show some connection—"

"You think there is one, then?" said his uncle swiftly, and did not wait for a reply. "In that case, I must point out to you that what happened last night was a direct result of your meddling."

"Well . . . perhaps. The reaction was rather quick for that." He paused a moment, and then said, "Unless it had been arranged beforehand—" drawing out the words, and making no attempt to explain what he meant.

Sir Nicholas gave him an exasperated look. "I suppose you think you've got an idea," he said. And then, still sharply, "I thought you liked sole cardinal, Jenny. You're only playing with your food."

"I was just thinking," said Jenny.

"What, in heaven's name?"

"He offered once not to meddle again . . . ever. Over and above the normal exercise of his profession, I mean." Her tone had an unaccustomed sharpness, and Antony glanced at her uneasily.

"Then why don't you hold him to it?" demanded Sir Nicholas, with not unreasonable indignation.

"If I remember rightly," said Antony, trying to lighten an atmosphere that had become a little tense, "she changed the subject by telling me she loved Geoffrey Horton."

"I do not feel that the subject of marital infidelity is a fit matter for jest," his uncle told him austerely.

"I didn't say I was in love with him," Jenny pointed out. "I said I loved him *but*."

"That seems a little inconsequent, even for you," said Sir Nicholas, unappeased.

"I only meant—"

She was still explaining, and Sir Nicholas was looking harassed, when Gibbs arrived with the dessert. It is probable that none of them had really enjoyed the meal.

III

By early afternoon the evening papers had come out with the story—rather garbled—of the holdup, and the subsequent arrest of one Robert Nolan. Johnny Lund phoned at about three o'clock, more querulous than sympathetic.

"I can't think what you're up to."

Antony counted to ten, reminded himself that his young friend was worried, and replied mildly enough. "Not my idea, Johnny. In fact, you could have knocked me down with a feather."

"It isn't funny," said Johnny resentfully.

"No. It isn't the end of the world, either. Have Cobbold's come up with anything yet?"

"If you mean about Danny Owen,"—which is what should be interesting you, his tone declared—"not a thing."

"Owen, or Lucas, or my dear friend Oscar Whitehead."

"I'm sorry."

"Never mind. There was one other item—"

"They've found the *Hazard Club* chauffeur, if that's what you mean."

"That's good."

"Not really. He's an elderly man called Carver, and he drives and services the car, and helps out with odd jobs between whiles. Does that help you?"

"That rather depends. Did anyone talk to him?"

"Yes, they did. He doesn't always drive the car, has no idea who takes it out when he doesn't, has never driven Paul Granville."

"I see what you mean. *Not* helpful. All right, Johnny, I'll be in touch."

Meg and Roger arrived at teatime, both of them demanding details of the story. "If you've come to say I told you so," said Antony disagreeably, "you may save your breath."

"I don't need to say it, do I?" Roger asked, but Meg was more inclined to belligerence.

"Darling, I do think it's too bad of you. It isn't as if you could do Lynn any good."

"That, d-darling," said Maitland, who only used the endearment when he was thoroughly irritated, "is a m-matter of opinion."

"I should have thought it was obvious."

"Not to me."

"But, Antony—" He could see that she was really upset, and was amused and touched when she sought to hide it by looking around for another source of grievance. "You're encouraging Roger in bad habits, what's more."

"If you mean that he's getting a taste for gambling—"

"You shouldn't mind, Meg," Jenny told her. "After all, he won."

"It's the principle of the thing," said Meg, who had still, under her affectations, a good many of the inhibitions inherent in her upbringing. But she smiled at Antony to show there was no real ill feeling.

"What are you going to do next?" Roger asked.

"Wait till we get into court, I suppose." He hesitated, and then said as though unwillingly, "I'm worried about Johnny, as well as about Lynn Edison. I don't see my way."

But the next move came long before that . . . on the following day, to be precise. . . .

He recognized Whitehead's voice as soon as he heard it on the telephone. "Maitland here," he said, and was aware of excitement. "What can I do for you?"

"A problem I've run into. Nothing very important. I think you could help me."

"If you want legal advice, you ought to see a solicitor." He wasn't quite sure what he would have done if Whitehead had accepted this suggestion.

"These distinctions." The telephone accentuated his drawl almost to the point of caricature. "A flat voice," Lynn Edison had said, and that might be fair enough, though it was odd she hadn't recognized . . . "I'd rather see you first, if you don't mind," Whitehead was saying.

"If you prefer."

"Always a good thing to have a friend at court." He chuckled as he spoke, so that Antony was nearly deafened and held the receiver indignantly away from his ear. "Can I see you tomorrow?"

"I shall be in chambers all day."

"I don't suppose you've got that place of yours bugged, have you?"

"I don't suppose so either."

"Then . . . would eleven o'clock suit you?"

"Excellently well."

Jenny was sitting in her favorite corner of the sofa, with a book on her lap. He smiled at her as he replaced the receiver, and for the first time he could remember received a stony look in return. "I'm going to see Whitehead tomorrow, in chambers," he told her.

"I thought it was something like that." She paused, and added, still unsmiling, "Even the back of your neck looked excited."

He came back to the fire. "You ought to be pleased, love. If anything breaks, it ought to help Lynn Edison."

"I don't believe that."

"But it's true."

"You may think so, nobody else does. Don't you see, Antony, all this business about the Mafia, and American gangsters, and everything . . . it's nothing to do with Lynn?"

"It's to do with Granville. He's the one who's dead."

"If he was helping them, why should they have killed him? Lynn had the best of motives—"

"She didn't do it."

"You say she didn't, but I think I'd rather believe in intuition than in this ridiculous reason of yours."

"I thought you believed her."

"Well, perhaps she didn't do it after all. Danny Owen has a motive too . . . a financial motive. Uncle Nick always says that's more convincing than anything else. Anyway, I don't believe there's any connection—"

"Jenny love, not you too?"

"What do you mean?"

He was conscious of a feeling of hopelessness. He said, carefully, "I've relied on your forbearance for too long."

"I've never minded what you did . . . when there was a reason. But this time there is no reason, only you're too stubborn to see it."

He was getting angry now. "I may be wrong," he said. "But —you must see this, Jenny—I've got to be s-sure."

"It won't make any difference, to lose your temper," said Jenny, and lowered her eyes again deliberately to her book.

He moved then, covering the space between them in a couple of strides, and grabbed her wrists and jerked her upright, so that her hands lay between his and against his chest. The book slid unheeded to the floor. "I've had enough of this," he said. "What do you want? I'll do anything you say." When she did not reply he added angrily, "Shall I phone Whitehead and tell him I c-can't meet him, after all?"

"Antony . . . no!"

"What do you want then?"

"I don't want you to do anything that would make you—that would make you despise yourself."

"I see. But you think I'm wrong."

"Yes, I do think that. Besides—" she hesitated, and then went on in a shaken voice, "I'm frightened."

He released her wrists then, and put his arms around her. After a pause, "I rather think I'm frightened too," he said, with an attempt at lightness. And then, "But you've always known that, haven't you?"

This time Jenny did not attempt to reply.

It wasn't until much later that he remembered that Whitehead hadn't asked for any directions as to how to reach Sir Nicholas's chambers in the Inner Temple. On consideration, he decided it was obvious that the American would already have made himself familiar with his destination.

MONDAY, *11th March*

I

Afterward, the taxi driver's evidence was clear. He had driven a fare—an American gentleman he had taken him to be—from Bayswater Road to the point where the Strand becomes Fleet Street, and had seen him, before he himself could turn into Chancery Lane, starting to cross the road.

The bus driver's evidence was even more to the point. He had been stopped by the traffic almost opposite Temple Bar, and had watched a tall man weaving his way across the road between the stationary cars, and trucks, and taxis. When the man was in front of the bus he stopped suddenly, and then fell backward. No, the bus hadn't been in motion, he'd swear he never touched him.

Of the passers-by, only two remained on the scene. The others hurried on their way, insensible of the fact that drama had touched their lives. The man who stayed, a doctor, went immediately to the fallen man. He had not heard anything out of the way, had prematurely diagnosed a heart attack, and was startled to find that his patient had been shot, neatly, between the eyes. The woman who stayed listened to his story, and produced a highly-colored tale of bullets that fanned her cheek, and a man in black who wormed his way with sinister speed through the crowd on the pavement.

The policeman who had materialized only a few minutes after the event listened to her indulgently, took down her name and address, and managed, somehow, to send her on her way. By this time another crowd had gathered, who this time showed no signs of dispersing.

All Maitland knew at that point was that Oscar Whitehead hadn't arrived on time. But it wasn't the prospect of the visit that was distracting his attention from the papers he was working on, but the thought of Jenny, with all her defenses down at last. . . .

He rang Whitehead's flat, as in duty bound, at eleven-thirty, and got no reply. Whitehead was on his way, or he'd changed his mind again. Either way, did it really matter? He sent out for sandwiches and went on working during the luncheon hour, not very effectively. And at two o'clock Hill rang through to say apologetically that Chief Inspector Conway would like to see him. Sometimes he thought that Hill had been born apologizing.

"You may have trouble with Conway," Sykes had said, and the detective looked like trouble when he marched in, stiff as a ramrod, and stood by the desk, ignoring Maitland's greeting.

"You had an appointment with a man named Whitehead this morning."

"What of it?"

Conway ignored the question. "What was your business with him?"

"I haven't the faintest idea. No, really, Chief Inspector . . . the appointment was made at his instigation."

"But you've seen him, haven't you, several times? And formed some half-baked theory—"

"I don't think my theories have anything to do with you."

"You were warned, in this case, what would come of your interfering, and now see what's happened!"

"As a matter of interest . . . what?"

"Whitehead was shot through the head, in the Strand in broad daylight, at three minutes past eleven this morning."

"What?" said Maitland again. This time he sounded startled. He left his place behind the desk and walked to the window and stood looking out. "You'd better sit down, Chief Inspector. This may take some time."

"What have you to tell me?" He sat down, as directed, but the stiffness had not left his manner. After a moment Maitland came back to his chair again.

"Only, in a little more detail, what I have thought about Granville, and Whitehead, and the *Hazard Club*."

"Before we go any further, I think you should know what brought me here this morning."

"Why . . . the appointment. I assumed you'd found some note—"

"I guessed Whitehead was coming here from the contents of his pockets. He had in his wallet a certified check for five thousand pounds, payable to you."

"I . . . *what*?"

"A certified check for five thousand pounds, payable to you," said Conway again, unamiably. "So what I really want to know, Mr. Maitland, is what would the consideration have been?"

"I haven't—I told you this—I haven't the faintest idea."

"I see."

"Unless—you'll have thought of this for yourself, of course—unless I was right in my surmises and he wanted to buy me off."

"Yes, I had got as far as that. The question is, what made him think he could?"

"Nothing that I have ever said to him, I can assure you of that."

"No, you have been motivated throughout solely by concern for your client," said Conway sarcastically. "Even though it seemed unlikely that your efforts could be of any help to her."

"Now, I-look here, Chief Inspector—"

"Wouldn't you say my questions were reasonable ones, Mr. Maitland?"

"Reasonable or not, they're d-damned insulting."

"I am afraid I cannot accept responsibility for that." As Maitland's anger intensified, Conway became more relaxed. Antony got up, and took another turn to the window and back.

"It looks like a gang killing . . . don't you think?"

"Of course I do. But what I do want to know—and I think I have a right to insist on an answer, Mr. Maitland—is, what is your part in all this?"

"I'm acting for Lynn Edison . . . remember?"

"But this can be of no concern to her affairs."

"That's a matter of opinion. I happen to think—"

"Yes, you were going to tell me that, weren't you?"

"I think . . . I thought . . . I don't know what to think now. Heaven and earth, if Whitehead was the king pin, as I've thought him, who bumped him off?"

"I gather you yourself have an alibi." Conway almost smiled as he said this, but Antony was in no mood for pleasantries.

"Either I was blackmailing him, or I murdered him," he declared. "You can't have it both ways."

"No," said Conway, with a show of regret. He seemed to be enjoying himself now. "But you were going to tell me—"

"Well . . . if you like." He sounded oddly unsure of himself. "I'm bound to say that now that Whitehead's dead—"

"Never mind that."

"All right then. Let's start with Paul Granville buying the *Hazard Club* and finding that it didn't do quite as well as he expected and that the mortgage payments were difficult to meet. Then Whitehead comes over, prospecting . . . do you think that's unlikely, Chief Inspector?"

"It has happened, lately, in more instances than this," said Conway in a grudging tone.

"Very well. He's looking for cover, and what better front could he have than Paul Granville . . . a popular star . . . a family favorite. So he pays off the mortgage, and in return Granville is only too glad to let him use the Club's facilities, nominate its employees, and so on. As part of the deal Granville makes a will in favor of Danny Owen; Owen may have known nothing of the circumstances, but he could be trusted to play ball if the occasion should arise. The bank robberies which have been carried out so ruthlessly are almost certainly part of the subsequent operations; the link there is Eddie Baker, who left a fingerprint in the getaway car on one occasion, and who 'sometimes drove for Paul Granville' according to his girl."

"So much," said Conway, "I can swallow without too much difficulty."

"It's the next bit that's difficult . . . I know. I think Granville killed Cynthia Edison, who really seems to have had very little reason for taking her own life, and if I have to make a guess at the reason I should say that, living in intimacy with him as she did, she had come to know, or suspect, something of the Club's activities. I think, in all probability, that Whitehead ordered her death for this reason, but Granville was the obvious person to carry it out."

"You still have to explain why Miss Edison didn't tell Granville, or any of her friends, about the part in *The Silent City.*"

"I can think of half a dozen possible explanations, but I don't know which one—if any—is true. Anyway, the real point at issue is Granville's death, isn't it?"

"It certainly is."

"Well, I think Lynn Edison really received the phone call she spoke of; I think Whitehead made it deliberately to get her to Granville's flat. I think she was framed."

"Come now, Mr. Maitland, I can see you suggesting that in court. But here, between the two of us—"

"I can't compel your belief."

"Tell me, then, who killed Granville . . . and why?"

"Whitehead, or Owen, it doesn't really matter. Certainly, Owen's arrival so shortly after Miss Edison got there was not fortuitous. As for the reason, Granville had shown he didn't like questions about the *Hazard Club,* and I should have certainly returned to the subject after the weekend recess. You'll agree they've shown they know how to be ruthless, and if they weren't sure how much he might give away—"

"None of this is proof, Mr. Maitland, and you know it."

"I don't believe the girl killed him."

"And now Whitehead, too, is dead. Can you suggest any reason for that?"

"Someone who knew he was coming here this morning. Someone who wanted to prevent him—" He broke off, and shrugged angrily. "I don't know. It doesn't seem to make any sense at all."

"I'm not denying you've embarrassed them, Mr. Maitland, by your activities. If Whitehead wanted to buy you off, somebody may have felt that was a rash, or an unnecessary step to take. Do you want police protection?"

"No. No, I don't."

"I think, if I were you, I should be very careful."

"It would be cheaper to kill me than to bribe me, certainly."

"Exactly. Can I rely on you, at least, to behave with some discretion?"

"I don't know."

"You're not doing Miss Edison any good by all this, you know."

"Unfortunately, that's true. But if something comes up . . . no, Chief Inspector, I can't promise anything."

"You're very stubborn."

Jenny had said that, hadn't she? Wouldn't it be easier just to forget the whole thing, leave Lynn Edison's affairs to Johnny Lund, and eventually to Uncle Nick's pleading? He felt tired suddenly, tired of the whole wretched business. But if any opportunity arose. . . .

Perhaps it was fortunate that he couldn't foresee at that moment just what form the "opportunity" would take.

When he got home that evening, Jenny wasn't there.

II

At first he didn't think anything of it. She had been out somewhere in the car, perhaps, and been caught in a traffic jam on the way home. But after a while he telephoned the garage where Jenny, as one of the owner's favorites, was allowed to leave the car, and was told the Jaguar was there, it hadn't been out all day.

He went downstairs then, to find Gibbs hovering at the back of the hall. "Did Mrs. Maitland say where she was going?"

"I was not aware that Mrs. Maitland was still out."

"You saw her go, then. Did she say where?"

"To the shops, Mr. Maitland, at about two o'clock. Naturally, I assumed she had returned."

"She isn't with Mrs. Stokes, I suppose."

"I should have been bound to see her if she had gone downstairs."

Back to his own quarters, to look for the bag that Jenny usually carried on a shopping expedition. The hook in the kitchen was empty. He went down to the study then, to find, as he had feared, that Sir Nicholas was far readier to revert to the question of Conway's visit to chambers that afternoon than he was to discuss his niece's disappearance. "Good heavens, Antony, Jenny must have some life of her own. You can't expect her always to be waiting on your convenience."

"But if she went out at two o'clock—"

"She is having tea with some chance-met friend," said Sir Nicholas didactically.

But by ten o'clock, when still she hadn't returned, he was almost as concerned as his nephew, and volunteered to telephone the hospitals while Antony called the police.

The constable who came around in response to his call was polite and sympathetic, but obviously unimpressed by any sense of urgency. "Some message has gone astray," he said comfortably. "That'll be it, you'll find." And then, what was obviously a routine question, "Had there been any argument?"

He couldn't quite bring himself to the lie. "Well, yes, there was, in a way." It was so obvious to anyone who knew her that Jenny wouldn't do anything out of pique, but it was also obvious that the confession set the constable's mind completely at rest.

"You ring some of your friends, sir. You'll find that's where she'll be."

"I've already done that."

"Give her time to get over it, sir. She'll be back."

Roger arrived just as the representative of the law was leaving. "What's all this about Jenny?" he asked, following Antony into the hall.

"She went out at two o'clock, and we haven't seen her since."

"Have you tried—?"

"Everything we can think of." He turned his head as his uncle came out of the study.

"No accident," said Sir Nicholas. "That's something to be thankful for, at any rate."

"Is it?" said Antony. "I'm not so sure."

"What are you thinking?"

"That somebody shot Whitehead—"

"I didn't know that," said Roger.

"This morning, on his way to see me. That isn't the point. Whoever shot him may have an equal reason for wanting to shut my mouth."

"That sounds as if you knew—"

"If Jenny's been kidnapped, that itself gives me ideas . . . don't you see?"

"It's too early to talk—"

"No, it isn't. Sykes warned me, and Conway warned me. But I never thought of this, you see."

"What are you going to do?"

"What can I do? Wait." He thought as he spoke how often Jenny had waited. . . .

"You'll let me know if—"

156

"I will, of course. But now, if you don't mind, both of you, I'd rather be alone."

<h1 style="text-align:center">III</h1>

He saw Roger out and lingered on the step a moment. It was a cold night, with a feeling of damp in the air. When he came back into the house again the study door was shut. He went upstairs slowly.

But once he was back in the big living room, where everything spoke to him of Jenny, he moved without any hesitation at all. The phone book first, then the telephone. He muttered the number to himself as he dialed it, afraid of getting it wrong. The brief pause while the bell shrilled unanswered seemed an eternity, and then the voice that spoke sounded unfamiliar, so that he said cautiously, "Mr. Lucas?"

"Speaking."

"Antony Maitland here. I want to see you."

"Isn't that rather irregular?" The voice sounded amused, but indulgent. Antony brushed the objection aside.

"I think you know why."

"Indeed I do. You will forgive me for pointing out, Mr. Maitland, that this call of yours has confirmed my own suspicions—"

"Yes, of course." He sounded impatient.

"How very impetuous of you. Now, I hadn't meant to call you until tomorrow. I suppose you would like to know where your wife is spending the night."

"You suppose correctly." It was hard to speak at all for the anger that shook him, but somehow he must keep calm.

"I'm afraid I can't tell you. There are certain preliminaries—"

"I understand all that."

"Are you alone?"

"Of course," he said again, curtly.

"It is a little late to be paying calls, but perhaps in the circumstances you would like to come here to see me."

"I should like nothing better."

"Very well. My flat is three twenty . . . turn left when you leave the lift."

Antony replaced the receiver. His hand was not quite steady. The room was very quiet now, and the silence seemed like a reproach. Lucas was so sure of himself he didn't even feel the need to threaten . . . and how right he was. The thing now was to get out of the house without Uncle Nick hearing him. . . .

IV

Sir Nicholas also was making a phone call. He was speaking to the Assistant Commissioner of Police (Crime), whom he knew only slightly. "I hesitate to disturb you at this time of night, Sir Edwin,"—which was a lie—"but I am seriously worried about the disappearance of my niece, Jenny Maitland."

"Antony Maitland's wife?" The Assistant Commissioner sounded startled . . . the implications of which were not lost upon Sir Nicholas, though he spoke as smoothly as ever.

"That is correct. She went out at two o'clock, and has not been home since."

"Have you—?"

"The local police are of the opinion that it is a voluntary disappearance; I may add that it is entirely reasonable that they should think so at this stage. But I am afraid that in view of my nephew's activities—"

"Yes," said the Assistant Commissioner. "Yes, I see."

"If Chief Inspector Sykes were not in hospital I should not be troubling you."

"Let's get this straight, Sir Nicholas." The Assistant Commissioner prided himself on being a plain, blunt man. "You're suggesting that Mrs. Maitland has been kidnapped."

"Yes."

"And that the fact is somehow connected with the case in which your nephew has been—er—"

"Meddling," said Sir Nicholas succinctly.

"—with which he has been concerning himself."

"Precisely."

"He believes that the bank robberies we are investigating are in some way concerned with the death of Paul Granville."

"I have to admit I do not agree with him. But his own inquiries will be no less of annoyance to the—to the gang," said Sir Nicholas, doing violence to his feelings, but unable to think of a more appropriate word.

"The man you want is Conway," said the Assistant Commissioner, very positively.

"I am afraid that Chief Inspector Conway is not altogether persuaded of my nephew's good faith."

"Oh, surely—"

"His attitude may not be considered entirely without justification," said Sir Nicholas stiffly, "but at the moment I find it inconvenient."

"I think you will find it is no more than dislike for what he regards as interference."

"That is not my impression. In view of everything that has happened—"

"I am aware that there have been occasions in the past when Mr. Maitland's assistance has not been altogether appreciated."

"I am speaking of something rather more serious than that," said Sir Nicholas flatly.

"And I'm sure you're wrong. Nobody at the Yard has any doubt of his integrity."

"Then let me say, Sir Edwin—if I may do so without offending you—that at times this confidence is expressed in rather an odd way."

"I assure you—" He was beginning to sound harassed now. Sir Nicholas interrupted him smoothly.

"Very well, I must accept your assurance. But at the moment I am extremely anxious. I don't know what he has in mind, but I am very much afraid he may do something rash."

"If he has any information—"

"Now, that is just what I am complaining of. You people

would be the first to grumble if he were to insist on confiding in you every idea that comes into his head."

"Shall I speak to Conway?" said the Assistant Commissioner, throwing in his hand.

"I was hoping you would offer to do so. Let me repeat, the attitude of the local police was completely reasonable, from their point of view, but I do feel that inquiries should be put in hand without delay."

"I will take the matter up immediately."

But when Sir Nicholas went upstairs to his nephew's quarters there was no answer to his knocking, and when he pushed the door open and went in the rooms were empty and silent. He thought, sadly, that it felt as if Jenny had been away for a very long time, but then another idea occurred to him and he went downstairs again rather quickly and pulled open the bottom left-hand drawer of his desk.

The automatic pistol with which he had provided himself after a certain lively night five years before was no longer in its accustomed place.

V

Maitland had been lucky in finding a cab quickly, and reached Leinster Court within ten minutes of leaving home. He had a feeling he was being followed, but he hadn't time to bother about that, and in any case—considering his destination —it was a waste of the shadow's time.

Leinster Court offers luxury, and demands in return a higher-than-average rent from its tenants. It should have occurred to him before that it was a strange place to find the manager even of one of the larger London banks. But there again, the man might have money of his own—presumably Head Office thought so—or he might, in choosing his luxuries, put the holding of a good address at the top of the list. Vincent Lucas occupied one of the medium-sized flats, and there was no sign that in furnishing it he had been motivated by economy.

He came to the door himself, very promptly, in response to

Antony's ring. "A very great pleasure, I have been wanting to renew our acquaintance."

Maitland came in, and pushed the door shut behind him, and stood leaning back against it. He said without preamble, "Where is she?"

"Not here. Surely you did not think I should be so indiscreet. My wife, lucky woman, is in the south of France, but even so—"

Perhaps it was the casual tone that infuriated him further. He felt the bile rise in his throat, and swallowed impatiently. "I still want to know where she is."

"Don't distress yourself, my dear fellow. She has taken no harm."

"I hope," said Antony, "for you sake, that that's true."

"It is, I assure you. But come in and make yourself comfortable. You must be cold, coming out without a coat on a night like this." He led the way into a pleasant, masculine room, and waved invitingly at a deep arm chair. "Let me get you something to drink."

Maitland took the chair, the warmth flowed over him like a blessing. "What are you offering me?" he asked. "A Mickey Finn?"

"My dear fellow! Nothing so crude. In any case, I want to talk to you. Hadn't you realized that?"

"I thought perhaps"—it was queer how tired he was—"I thought perhaps your purpose had been served merely by my coming here."

"No." Lucas was busy at a table at the side of the room, as casual still as if this was a friendly encounter. "Water, or soda, or would you perhaps like it neat?"

"Water, please." It was extraordinary how conventional politeness persisted at a time like this. But he disregarded the glass when it was placed at his elbow, and leaned forward, his hands between his knees. "You're going to tell me your terms, I suppose. Can't you just do it, and cut out the palaver."

"There is really no hurry. First, I want to make something

161

very clear to you. You may be tempted to violence, but if any harm comes to me I think it very unlikely that you will see your wife again." He sat down, and raised his glass. "To your good health, Mr. Maitland. To your continued good health."

"You've got me here now. I suppose that's what you wanted. Can't you let her go?"

"I don't want to kill you, Mr. Maitland—"

"That's b-bloody nice of you!"

"—there has been too much killing already."

"I am in blood stepped in so far—"

"Really, I find that . . . almost offensive."

"Do you though?"

"Yes. However, I am willing to make allowances. But don't you think we could talk more comfortably if you got rid of the gun in your pocket?"

"On the whole, I feel happier with it there."

"So you *are* armed. How very melodramatic of you! I see I was right to issue my warning, but you cannot, you really cannot have thought I should be so naive as to give instructions for your wife's release and leave myself at your mercy."

"I hoped . . . that's all." But even that wasn't true. He had succeeded in involving Jenny (and Jenny had been angry with him for almost the first time he could remember), and now the only thing that mattered was getting her safely away. He was concentrating on this thought rather fiercely. For himself he had no hope at all, and he was too tired even to care.

"Come now," said Lucas persuasively. "If you will put it on the table over there we can get down to business." There was something inflexible behind the mild manner of speaking. Antony hesitated, but only for a moment. He got up and walked across to the side table and put down Sir Nicholas's pistol beside a bottle of White Horse.

"There!" he said. "Can we talk now?"

"If you will go back to your chair again. That's better," he added encouragingly, as Maitland obeyed. "I was right—wasn't I?—in thinking that you reconized me that day in court."

"Yes. Where I went wrong was in thinking that you couldn't possibly recognize me."

"Why should I not?"

"You were in a group I was studying. I was alone. Besides, in my wig—"

"I think perhaps your appearance is more distinctive than you realize, Mr. Maitland. I was also right in thinking that, at that point, there was no very great harm done."

"Quite right."

"What first made you suspect—?"

"Well, after that chap of yours held me up in the square I began to wonder if Whitehead was really alone in running the show. It couldn't have been reaction from my second visit to the *Hazard Club*; I didn't think he'd had a chance to give the order, and besides there hadn't really been time."

"On your first visit Eddie Baker reacted even more quickly."

"Yes, but look what happened to him. It was only later that it occurred to me that the holdup might have been prearranged, not by Whitehead. If he'd been responsible I thought he'd have been at pains to call it off when I arrived at the club."

"That is all quite clear. But what led you to me?"

"Two things: first, that you were the only person I could think of who might be afraid of *my* inquiries, as opposed to any that the police might make."

"After I gave evidence at the libel trial all the world and his wife knew that I had been once to the *Hazard Club*."

"Yes, but I'd seen you there, and might well have drawn my own conclusions from the way you behaved toward Granville. And so I did, but at first I only thought you were helping him out because he had to prove damage."

"You said, two things, Mr. Maitland."

"The second was that Whitehead knew altogether too much about you, and your alleged motives, when I mentioned you to him." He paused, and then said rather tentatively, "Can't we—?"

163

"Before we go into the question of my terms for Mrs. Maitland's release, I want you to tell me exactly what you know."

"But—"

"I'm afraid I'm quite determined about it, my dear fellow. For my own instruction . . . for my protection even."

"Will you tell me, first, how you managed to lay your hands on Jenny?"

"Very well. It was really quite simple."

"She wouldn't have fallen for anything like a fake message. I'm sure of that."

"I haven't the pleasure of her acquaintance, but I felt reasonably sure of that, too. No, a car drove up beside her and the passenger in the back seat leaned out to ask her the way. It was a little odd, perhaps, to open the door instead of winding down the window, but I don't suppose she thought anything of that. In any event, she stepped toward the car to speak to him more easily . . . he had only to reach out a hand to her wrist and jerk her inside. It was all over in a moment, none of the passers-by noticed anything wrong. I don't suppose she even had time to feel frightened."

"What do you mean?"

"It was necessary to drug her, of course."

"Of course." But he couldn't think of Jenny, daren't think of her now. And there was Lucas talking again, his voice quietly insistent.

"You will remember, you were going to tell me—"

It required an effort to cast his mind back to the beginning of the affair. "Granville killed Cynthia Edison, didn't he? At your . . . I suppose at your instigation."

"As to that, I think it was Whitehead he was more afraid of. A man of ability, but not much imagination. And indiscreet. It was the least he could do to make amends."

"I see."

"He was fantastically jealous, you know, of her success in landing a part in some play or other. He seemed to regard stage success as in some way more desirable than success in the films or in television. I think that almost reconciled him to what he had to do."

"So that's why she didn't tell her friends. She told him, though he denied it, and then she wanted him to have time to get used to the idea."

"Your guess is as good as mine, Mr. Maitland."

"How did you first come to be mixed up with Granville and Whitehead?" Antony asked, and for the first time drank from the glass at his elbow.

"That's a long story."

"All the same, I should like to know."

"Well, if you wish. I was looking around at the time for an additional source of revenue. The bank's salary scale is not really as generous as one could wish. We held a mortgage on the Club, you know, and then it was suddenly paid off—that made me think, I can tell you, knowing Paul's financial circumstances as I did. And then, equally suddenly, Whitehead was always underfoot. So I cut myself in on the game, it wasn't really difficult. Paul was in some ways a simple soul, easily bluffed. And Whitehead foresaw certain advantages. I think I may say we both profited from the association."

"In what way?"

"You're very curious all of a sudden. Perhaps I should remind you that you're not going to be in a position to use this information."

"Even so—"

"There is no harm in telling you, of course. I learned from Whitehead to be completely ruthless, when it became necessary for my own safety. No one can say I didn't learn the lesson well. He learned from me details of bank procedure. I had hoped also a certain subtlety, but that it seems was beyond his grasp."

"You killed Granville—"

"To be exact, that was a task that Whitehead undertook."

"—because you thought he might give something away under cross-examination."

"You remember, I am sure, that I was in court when Paul was giving his evidence."

"I do. And it was your idea, I imagine, in view of what you tell me, to implicate Lynn Edison."

"It was," said Lucas, with a measure of satisfaction evident in his tone. "I thought it would make you lose interest in the girl."

"It might have done, if Whitehead hadn't made the telephone call. Why was it arranged like that?"

"Because both Danny Owen and I had given evidence in court and might have been recognized. Even if she recognized the caller as an American, it didn't seem to matter much."

"It did, as a matter of fact, but only because I was already suspicious of him. To go back a little, why was Eddie Baker killed?"

"That was Whitehead's doing. Eddie was out to make an impression, and never stopped to consider that an attack on you might be foolish, at that time and in that place. Whitehead's reaction was also over-quick. It made me wonder whether, perhaps, our association hadn't gone on long enough. Though once Eddie was dead he was right to take care of the girl too, of course. Anything else would have been in the nature of unfinished business."

"But why, in the long run . . . you killed him, didn't you?"

"I gave the order, certainly."

Maitland waved this aside as irrelevant. "Why did you decide to do it *then*?"

"Because he made the mistake, Mr. Maitland, of believing you could be bribed. He was wrong, wasn't he?"

"Yes, he was wrong." He added, thoughtfully, *"The attempt and not the deed confounds us."*

"That is exactly what I thought," said Lucas cordially. "But it was too good an idea to waste altogether. With certain refinements—"

"I don't quite see—"

"It will serve the purpose very well. I have in my pocket a certified check for—five thousand pounds I think was the sum

166

he had in mind. You are going to accept it, it would be nice to think with becoming gratitude."

"But, I—"

"If you don't I shall have to kill you, of course. Oh, not here, not now. How inconvenient that would be. But I have only to give the order and you will not reach home alive."

"I must congratulate you on the effectiveness of your arrangements."

"Yes, they are effective. In the unhappy event of your refusing to accept the check I shall also—very regretfully, my dear fellow—arrange for Mrs. Maitland's demise."

"I s-see."

"Let me explain to you the safeguards I have in mind. You will also call off the police . . . am I right in thinking you communicated with them?"

"Quite right."

"Well, you will say you have heard from your wife—you had a quarrel, perhaps, and she has gone to a hotel, but she wouldn't tell you where. I am sure a man of your ingenuity can make up some tale that will satisfy them. Then after a week—or a fortnight, perhaps—she will return home, very little the worse for wear, and I think you will be able to persuade her to corroborate whatever story you have told. And after *that,* Mr. Maitland, you will be quite at liberty to confide in the police what you know of my activities, for instance; but if you do there will be the little matter of the check to explain, and it will be a little late for explanations."

"I . . . see," said Antony again.

"I shall, of course, send someone to the bank with you, to see that the check is actually deposited. That, after all, is a natural precaution." He paused, smiling. "It is a good idea, don't you think?"

"I don't see why it is to your advantage to keep me alive."

"Because if you are killed there will be questions asked that may prove embarrassing."

"There are questions being asked already."

"Whitehead is dead . . . a gang killing. And no one believes you when you say that Paul's death is part of the same affair . . . am I right about that?"

"You are."

"The *Hazard Club* is being given up, of course, as a base for operations, and that, for your information, is the real reason that Whitehead had to die. He would never have agreed that it was an essential step for my own protection."

"Wait a bit! The three men who have been arrested . . . aren't you afraid they may give you away?"

"Fortunately no one knew of my complicity, except Paul, of course, and now Danny Owen. I think I am safe enough, and it occurs to me, Mr. Maitland, that I may find a use for you in the future . . . if some other business venture comes my way." He paused, and when Antony said nothing went on in a bracing tone. "Come now, you have heard my proposition. What have you got to say?"

"You don't give me much choice, do you?"

"Your life and Mrs. Maitland's as the price of your silence. It's a good bargain, isn't it?"

"I suppose so." He picked up his glass and drained it, and came quickly to his feet. "You wouldn't—if I gave you my word—let Jenny come home with me now?"

"My dear fellow! You must see I can't do that."

"Give me the check then." He went across and stood over Lucas, holding out his hand.

"Here you are. You have no qualms about this, I hope. You are, after all, leaving Lynn Edison to sink or swim."

"She can go to hell for all that I care." He stuffed the check into his pocket, and looked rather blankly at the glass he was still holding. "I think . . . if you've no objection I'll have another drink before I go." He was crossing the room as he spoke, still moving quickly, and he had put down the glass and picked up the pistol before the other man could say a word. "Now, Mr. Lucas, we'll play this my way for a change." He raised his voice a little and added, "You can come in now, Roger," and Roger

Farrell came into the room carrying, rather self-consciously, a large monkey wrench.

"I thought we might need this," he said.

"We may yet. No, keep still," he added, as Lucas shifted in his chair. "It would give me great pleasure to shoot you. Don't offer me the excuse."

"Are you mad? If Danny Owen doesn't hear from me—"

"He's not expecting to hear until tomorrow. You told me that yourself."

"Well . . . tomorrow—"

"—is also a good day. See if you can find something to tie him up with, Roger. We've no time to lose."

Roger, who was nothing if not resourceful, disappeared from the room, returning presently with a handkerchief, a silk scarf, and a pair of blue curtains which he proceeded to tear into strips. Vincent Lucas raged impotently until the gag was in place, the more so because neither of his captors took the slightest notice of him now, but continued their conversation over his head.

"Good of you to come," said Maitland, for all the world as though it were some normal, social occasion.

"You knew I would, didn't you? It must have been you who left the door unlatched."

"It was, of course. It didn't occur to me at first, but then I wondered if it might be you who was following."

"Why didn't you ask me—?"

"It was the only way I could get Uncle Nick off my neck," said Antony apologetically. "Can you imagine what he'd have said—?"

"I can form some vague idea."

"Well, there wasn't time for argument, you see."

"How soon did you know I was here?"

"Quite early on. I saw your shadow when I got up to put down the gun. I say, I hope you listened pretty carefully."

"I did. It was easy to see what you were after, so I made some notes as well." He held out his arm, so that Maitland could see the rather blurred writing that was scrawled on his cuff.

"If that isn't Exhibit No. 1, it ought to be," said Antony, admiringly.

"It seemed a good idea." Roger sounded gratified. "Do you think this will do? I don't think myself he's got a chance in a million of getting away."

Lucas was on the floor now, neatly trussed, and competently gagged. His eyes might have been the only thing alive about him, and they were very expressive. Antony regarded him with satisfaction, and pocketed the pistol. "That ought to hold him," he said. "Just make sure the telephone's out of order, will you?"

Roger wrenched the wires out of the wall. "I already took care of the one in the kitchen," he said. "Not that he has a hope in hell of getting through there. Come along now. If we shut this door, and then the outside one, nobody's likely to hear him bumping about."

"You know where we're going next?"

"To the *Hazard Club,* of course. Even I had worked that out."

"To fetch Jenny." He hesitated. "The thing is, Roger, I couldn't leave her there for one night, let alone for two weeks."

"Of course we couldn't."

"If she isn't there—"

"We come back here and try the effects of a little gentle persuasion, I suppose."

"Yes, but . . . do you realize you haven't once asked me what happens when we get to the Club?"

"We shall play it by ear. Is that what you mean?"

"Not exactly. There may be trouble."

"There's sure to be trouble," Roger corrected him cheerfully. "Come on."

VI

The doorman at the *Hazard Club* seemed to have some recollection of them; he let them in without question. This was better than Antony had expected, and he paused in the hall to take stock of the situation. Of the men who might try to stop them, only Danny Owen was known to them; but there might be others—perhaps many others—to whom they were known.

But for the moment there was no one to hinder them. In the first salon the *croupiers* were absorbed in their task, and there was the usual light-hearted babble of talk. In the baccarat room there was no one to notice whether they came or went, and in the supper room the waiters went about their work unheeding. They came back into the hall again to find it empty.

"Upstairs, I think," said Maitland. There was a calmness about him now, about which Roger was under no illusions at all. His mood was dangerous. They went together up the wide staircase. "Of course, they may have got her in the cellar," said Antony, still cool as ice. He did not add, "Or she may not be here at all," but the fear was beginning to take hold of him.

At the top of the stairs a man barred their way, a hefty looking chap in a lounge suit that looked too tight across the shoulders. "I'm sorry, sir, these upstairs rooms are private." The landing was wide, and carpeted in blue. There were four doors leading off it, solid, heavy doors.

"We want to see Mr. Owen," said Maitland, continuing his ascent, so that the man gave way a pace or two before him.

"I'm sorry, sir—" he said again. Antony took his hand from his pocket, and let him see the gun.

"Which room?" he asked. It occurred to Roger that he looked quite at home with the pistol in his hand, as though it was part of his normal equipment. The man who had intercepted them evidently thought so too; he gave one wild glance around him, as though seeking assistance, fell back a step, and waved a hand toward a door on their right. "Thank you," said Maitland, and gestured with the gun. "If you will precede us—"

Again the man obeyed, though he threw the door open with a violence that might have been in itself a warning. But when Maitland reached the doorway there was nothing out of the way to be seen . . . just Danny Owen, looking insignificant behind a wide, well-polished expanse of desk, and an elderly man who reminded Antony irresistibly of a colonel he had once known, and who was most probably one of the guests from downstairs.

"My name's Maitland." But as he spoke he saw from Danny Owen's appalled expression that he had no need to introduce himself. "I've come for my wife."

"I don't understand," said Owen, rallying his forces. And the other man said, "Really, sir, this is an outrage," for all the world as though he were really the colonel whom Maitland remembered.

"Don't tempt me," said Maitland, ignoring them both. "I'm just in the mood for a little target practice." He was standing well to the right of the doorway now. "Keep a lookout, Roger, will you?" he added. And then, to the man who had met them on the landing, "Get over there by the desk."

"What do you want?" asked Owen. His voice was higher pitched than it had been in court, and Antony felt a vicious pleasure at the tremor in it.

"I told you. My wife's here, isn't she? Are you going to tell me where to find her?"

"If your wife has a taste for gambling," said the colonel severely, "that's no reason for you to barge in like this, behaving like a maniac."

"It isn't quite as simple as that. Are you going to tell me?" he said again. Owen shook his head.

"I think you've gone mad," he said, but there was no conviction in his voice.

"Come here then." Owen hesitated, and then came slowly around the desk. The gun followed him until he reached the doorway, then Maitland said briskly, "Look after him, Roger, for a moment," and turned back to the two remaining men.

"Wait for us," he said, and found the key and transferred it to the outside of the door. "Perhaps I ought to warn you that if you try to get out, or create a disturbance, I shall certainly shoot Mr. Owen." He pulled the door shut behind him, and felt the key turn smoothly in the lock. "Now," he said. "Quickly!" And turned to see Roger releasing Owen from a sort of bear's hug in which he had enfolded him. "I think—" he went on, with the first hesitation he had shown. And then, more confidently, "Upstairs first."

This staircase was more narrow. They went up in single file, with Owen leading, and Roger bringing up the rear. Again there was the landing, but this one was uncarpeted; and the four doors, but these were less heavy than their counterparts on the floor below. Roger slipped past Owen and tried them each in turn. Only the one on the right, the one above the office, was locked. "This one," he said, standing back, and Maitland jammed the pistol in Danny Owen's ribs.

"All right. Open it." And heard as he spoke the sound of fists hammering on wood that drifted up from below. But it was too late to worry about that now.

Here, alone with his captors, even the small signs of bravado that Owen had shown downstairs had gone. He fumbled in his pocket and produced a large, old-fashioned key, and crossed the landing with Antony still close at his heels. The key rattled as he jammed it into the lock, and seemed for a moment to present some difficulty in turning. "Take this," said Maitland, thrusting the pistol into Roger's hand as the door swung open, and went quickly into the attic room beyond.

Jenny lay on the bed; an old-fashioned, iron bedstead, with mattress and pillows bare. Someone had taken off her overcoat and thrown a blanket over her. She was breathing deeply and evenly, as though in a heavy sleep, and her face was pallid and a little damp. Her curls clung damply about her forehead. He bent over her, taking her hand, and said, "Jenny, love—" in a voice that Roger had never heard before. Then he straightened, and looked at his friend, and went to take the pistol from him. His mouth was set in a hard line, and Roger relinquished the weapon with a distinct feeling of unease. But it was obvious which one of them would have to carry Jenny. Roger picked her up, blanket and all. She did not even stir, but lay in his arms limply.

The procession re-formed itself without any words being needed. Owen looked as if he might faint at any moment, and clung to the bannister as he went down the stairs. The banging from the office was deafening now; Maitland spared a moment to wonder which of the two prisoners was disregarding his threat. They might not have believed he meant it, but Danny Owen certainly did. Already there were people coming up the lower staircase. More guests, he thought. He caught up with Owen on the landing, and nudged him forward.

Afterward he thought it would have been sufficient if he had said, "This lady is ill, please let us pass," and hidden the gun from sight. But he had only one idea in his head just then—to get Jenny to a doctor—and he pursued it single-mindedly. He caught Owen's wrist with his left hand, and twisted his arm up painfully behind him. Then he let the three men on the staircase see the pistol. "We're in rather a hurry," he said. "Do you mind?" They backed away from him warily.

But this time the hall was by no means empty, it was milling with people, who threatened his plan by sheer force of numbers. If he tried to push through he could be disarmed from behind. There was a bunch of tough-looking customers, too, who had just come through the baize door at the back of the house. He halted on the fourth stair, and all of a sudden he wasn't cool any longer but uncomfortably near to panic. And while he sought for the words that would retrieve the situation—but surely it would need a miracle for that—the hammering from upstairs was echoed and then outdone by a thunderous knocking on the front door. Somebody went to tug it open, he thought it was one of the guests. . . .

. . . and three seconds later he found himself looking across the heads of the crowd at Chief Inspector Conway, and beyond him at the comfortable, familiar sight of uniformed police. He let Danny Owen go, and dropped the pistol back into his pocket. Someone came up and grabbed his arm, but he never noticed the fact, or the pain that shot through his shoulder.

"There'll be a police car," he said. "Will you take her home, Roger? I'll stay here, if I must."

It wasn't until he thought about it afterward that he realized that Chief Inspector Conway was looking pretty dazed himself.

TUESDAY, *12th March*

He sat by the bed, and waited for Jenny to come out of her coma. "Let her sleep it off," Dr. Prescott had said, adding callously, "She'll be none the worse for it. And it's no good looking blue murder at me, my boy," he had gone on with unimpaired cheerfulness. "I know what I'm talking about."

Antony had no choice but to believe him, but the time seemed very long.

It was nearly seven o'clock when she stirred, sighed deeply, and opened her eyes. She shut them again rather quickly, and he leaned forward to shade the light, and then saw that she had put out a hand, gropingly, to find his. "I knew you'd come," she said, and sighed again.

"Wake up, Jenny. You're at home."

"Am I? Am I really?" She opened her eyes, and this time kept them open, but they did not move far from his face. "Is everything all right, Antony? Are you all right?"

"Everything's fine."

176

"Were you right all the time? I mean . . . about Lynn, and everything."

"Partly right, anyway. Lynn will be released today. I left Johnny to look after all that; most appropriate, don't you think?"

Jenny wriggled a little, until she was more nearly in a sitting position. "Has he forgiven her for thinking—?"

"He's forgiven her. I gather he's feeling magnanimous, though rather annoyed not to have had a hand in last night's doings." He laughed suddenly, but his amusement had very little to do with what he was saying. "He's forgiven her, but I doubt if he'll ever let her forget. As for the rest of the mess," he added, not without satisfaction, "Inspector Conway has the thankless task of sorting that out, egged on by Uncle Nick and no less a person than the Assistant Commissioner. Shall I make you some tea?"

"Yes . . . no—"

"How are you feeling?"

"I've got a filthy taste in my mouth, and my head feels as if it's stuffed with cotton wool," said Jenny precisely. "But never mind that. I want to know what happened."

"What happened to you, love?"

"It's the silliest thing. A car stopped to ask the way, and that's all that I remember."

"They drugged you," said Antony, his expression bleak for a moment as he remembered Vincent Lucas, and his casual recounting of an enormity. "Didn't you come around at all?"

"Yes, once. At least, I don't think I was more than half awake. There was a man leaning over me, and I remember that he said, 'I hope for your sake you're on good terms with your husband,' and then he jabbed something into my arm, and everything started going around and around, and away and away—"

"That would be Danny Owen, damn him," said Antony with fervor.

"But you haven't told me—"

177

"Are you sure you feel well enough?"

"Quite sure."

He told her then, everything that he and Roger had done. He even told her about the constable who had asked if they'd had an argument. But he didn't tell her how he had felt, that was something for which he had no words. "And then there was Conway, turning up the doorstep at absolutely the right moment because Uncle Nick had been pulling strings," he concluded. "He didn't even have a search warrant, just the Assistant Commissioner's say-so, which offended his sense of propriety, of course."

"How did he know—?"

"Uncle Nick had guessed where they had taken you, just as Roger and I had done. And I must admit I've never been so glad to see anybody in my life before."

"What did Uncle Nick say when you got home?"

"Nothing, love. He was too bothered about you." He grinned at her, and Jenny smiled back, because when he looked like that she knew there was nothing more to worry about. "But I should think he'll excel himself when he sees the papers this morning."

It was perhaps as well for everybody concerned that the documents in a particularly fascinating case of defamation of title came into chambers that morning, effectively distracting Sir Nicholas's attention from his grievance.